The Satyr's Head
Tales of Terror

The Satyr's Head
Tales of Terror

Selected by David A. Sutton

Shadow Publishing

The Satyr's Head: Tales of Terror

First published as *The Satyr's Head & Other Tales of Terror*
by Corgi Books 1975

This edition © 2012 by David A. Sutton
Cover artwork & design © 2012 by Steve Upham

The Nightingale Floors © 1975 by James Wade
The Previous Tenant © 1975 by Ramsey Campbell
The Night Fisherman © 1975 by Martin I. Ricketts
Sugar and Spice and All Things Nice © 1975 by David A. Sutton
Provisioning © 1975 by David Campton
Perfect Lady © 1975 by Robin Smyth
The Business About Fred © 1975 by Joseph Payne Brennan
Aunt Hester © 1975 by Brian Lumley
A Pentagram for Cenaide © 1975 by Eddy C. Bertin
The Satyr's Head © 1975 by David A. Riley

The editor and publisher gratefully acknowledge the permission granted to
reproduce the copyright material in this book. Every effort has been made
to trace copyright holders and to obtain their permission for the use of
copyright material. The publisher apologises for any errors or omissions in
the above list and would be grateful if notified of any corrections that
should be incorporated in future reprints or editions of this book.

ISBN: 978-0-9539032-3-8

Shadow Publishing, 194 Station Road, Kings Heath,
Birmingham, B14 7TE, UK
david.sutton986@btinternet.com
http://davidasutton.co.uk

Acknowledgements

Special thanks to

~ Mike Ashley ~

~ Charles Black ~

~ Steve Upham ~

Contents

INTRODUCTION

D URING THE EARLY part of the 1970s I had begun editing and producing my fanzine *Shadow: Fantasy Literature Review*. This was in response to the numerous horror and fantasy fanzines then being devoted to film. And there was a lot happening on the literary side. *The Pan Book of Horror Stories* was in its middle age. The Ballantine Adult Fantasy Series had emerged in the mid-sixties, reprinting many classic works and later contemporary fantasy writers. Arkham House, having recently published *Thirty Years of Arkham House* in 1969, was to enter its most productive two decades, with something like seventy-plus titles from both contemporary, classic and "pulp" writers. Many paperback anthologies edited by August Derleth, Peter Haining and numerous others were popping up. The UK paperback publishers were all keen to have a horror genre line, thus Pan, Panther, Four Square, Sphere, Corgi, Fontana, Tandem, and so on all were bringing out horror series or one-off anthologies.

One of the paperback houses, Sphere Books, contacted me after seeing and being impressed with the copies of *Shadow Fantasy Literature Review* I had sent them. Their editor, Anthony Cheetham, commissioned me to edit a series of annual anthologies called *New Writings in Horror & the Supernatural*, exclusively to bring out previously unpublished tales of horror by new and well-known genre writers. On the other side of the coin, Sphere hired Richard Davis to edit the *Year's Best Horror Stories* series. Alas, Sphere backed away from *New Writings* after two volumes. *Year's Best* fared a little better, but was eventually dropped by Sphere. (Luckily it was

1

continued by Daw Books in the USA under editors Gerald W. Page from volume four and Karl Edward Wagner from volume eight). In 1972 I was busy compiling the contents for New Writings volume three when the expected contract failed to materialise...

With a batch of stories already to hand, I then contacted Corgi Books, a division of Transworld Publishers, and pitched to them a one-off anthology called The Satyr's Head & Other Tales of Terror. They liked the concept and the book was duly published in 1975 and quickly went out of print. Now, nearly forty years later here is The Satyr's Head: Tales of Terror, a new incarnation for a new generation of horror readers!

David A. Sutton
January 2012

THE NIGHTINGALE FLOORS

By James Wade

I

START TALKING ABOUT a broken-down old museum (one of those private collections set up years ago under endowments by some batty rich guy with pack-rat instincts) where strange things are supposed to happen sometimes at night, and people think you're describing the latest Vincent Price horror movie, or the plot of some corny Fu Manchu thriller, the kind that sophisticates these days call "campy" and cultivate for laughs.

But there are such places, dozens altogether I guess, scattered around the country; and you do hear some pretty peculiar reports about some of them once in a while.

The one I knew was on the South Side of Chicago. They tore it down a few years ago during that big urban renewal project around the university—got lawyers to find loopholes in the bequest, probably, and scattered the exhibits among similar places that would accept such junk.

Anyway, it's gone now, so I don't suppose there's any harm in mentioning the thing that went on at the Ehlers Museum in the middle 1950's. I was there, I experienced it; but how good a witness I am I'll leave up to you. There's plenty of reason for me to doubt my own senses, as you'll see when I get on with the story.

I don't mean to imply that everything in the Ehlers Museum was junk—far from it. There were good pieces in the armour collection, I'm told, and a few mummies in fair shape. The Remingtons were focus of an unusual gathering of early Wild West art, though some of them were said to be copies; I suppose even the stacks of quaint old posters had historical value in that particular field. It was because everything was so jammed together, so dusty, so musty, so badly lit and poorly displayed that the overall impression was simply that of some hereditary kleptomaniac's attic.

I learned about the good specimens after I went to work at the museum; but even at the beginning, the place held an odd fascination for me, trashy as it might have appeared to most casual visitors.

I first saw the Ehlers Museum one cloudy fall afternoon when I was wandering the streets of the South Side for lack of something better to do. I was still in my twenties then, had just dropped out of the university (about the fifth college I failed to graduate from) and was starting to think seriously about where to go from there.

You see, I had a problem—to be more accurate, I had a Habit. Not a major Habit, but one that had been showing signs lately of getting bigger.

I was one of those guys people call lucky, with enough money in trust funds from overindulgent grandparents to see me through life without too much worry, or so it seemed. My parents lived in a small town in an isolated part of the country, where my father ran the family industry; no matter to this story where or what it was.

I took off from there early to see what war and famine had left of the world. Nobody could stop me, since my money was my own as soon as I was twenty-one. I didn't have the vaguest notion what I wanted to do with myself, and that's probably why I found myself a Korean War veteran in Chicago at twenty-six with a medium-size monkey on my back, picked up at those genteel campus pot parties that were just getting popular then among the more advanced self-proclaimed sophisticates.

Lucky? I was an Horatio Alger story in reverse.

You see, although my habit was modest, my income was modest too, with the inflation of the forties and fifties eating into it. I had just come to the conclusion that I was going to have to get a job of

4

some kind to keep my monkey and me both adequately nourished. So there I was, walking the South Side slums through pale piles of fallen poplar leaves, and trying to figure out what to do, when I came across the Ehlers Museum, just like Childe Roland blundering upon the Dark Tower. There was a glass-covered signboard outside, the kind you see in front of churches, giving the name of the place and its hours of operation; and someone had stuck a hand-lettered paper notice on the glass that proclaimed, "Night Watchman Wanted. Inquire Within".

I looked up to see what kind of place this museum-in-a-slum might be. Across a mangy, weed-cluttered yard I saw a house that was old and big—even older and bigger than the neighbouring grey stone residences that used to be fashionable but now were split up into cramped tenement apartments. The museum was built of dull red brick, two and a half stories topped by a steep, dark shingled roof. Out back stood some sort of addition that looked like it used to be a carriage house, connected to the main building by a covered, tunnel-like walkway at the second storey level, something like a medieval drawbridge. I found out later that I was right in assuming that the place had once been the private mansion of Old Man Ehlers himself, who left his house and money and pack-rat collections in trust to preserve his name and civic Fame when he died, back in the late twenties. The neighborhood must have been fairly ritzy then.

The whole place looked deserted: no lights showed, though the day was dismally grey, and the visible windows were mostly blocked by that fancy art-nouveau stained glass that made Edwardian houses resemble funeral parlors. I stood and watched a while, but nobody went in or out, and I couldn't hear anything except the faint rattle of dry leaves among the branches of the big trees surrounding the place.

However, according to the sign, the museum should be open. I was curious, bored, and needed a job: no reason not to go in and at least look around. I walked up to the heavy, panelled door, suppressed an impulse to knock, and sidled my way inside.

"Dauntless, the slug-horn to my lips I set..."

II

The foyer was dark, but beyond a high archway just to the right I saw a big, lofty room lit by a few brass wall fixtures with gilt-lined black shades that made the place seem even more like a mortuary than it had from outside. This gallery must once have been the house's main living room, or maybe even a ballroom. Now it was full of tall, dark mahogany cases, glass-fronted, in which you could dimly glimpse a bunch of unidentifiable potsherds, stuck around with little descriptive placards.

The walls, here and all over the museum, were covered with dark red brocaded silk hangings or velvety maroon embossed wallpaper, both flaunting a design in a sort of fleur-de-lys pattern that I later learned was a coat of arms old Ehlers had dug up for himself, or had faked, somewhere in Europe.

The building looked, and smelled, as if nobody bad been there for decades. However, just under the arch stood a shabby bulletin board that spelled out a welcome for visitors in big alphabet-soup letters, and also contained a photo of the pudgy, mutton-chop bearded founder, along with a typed history of the museum and a rack of little folders that seemed to be guide-catalogues. I took one of these and, ignoring the rest of the notices, walked on into the first gallery.

The quiet was shy-making; for the first time in years, I missed Muzak. My footsteps, though I found myself almost tiptoeing, elicited sharp creaks from the shrunken floorboards, just as happens in the corridors of the Shogun's old palace at Kyoto, which I visited on leave during the Korean War. The Japs called those "Nightingale Floors", and claimed they had been installed that way especially to give away the nocturnal presence of eaves-droppers or assassins. The sound was supposed to resemble the chirping of birds, though I could never see that part of it.

I wondered what the reason was for Old Man Ehlers to have this kind of flooring. Just shrinkage of the wood from age, maybe. But then, he'd been around the world a lot in his quest for curios, probably. Maybe the idea for the floor really was copied from the Shogun's palace. But if so, why bother, since it wasn't the sort of relic that could be exhibited?

Anyway, I walked through that gallery without giving the specimens more than a glance. I understand that the Ehlers Collection of North American Indian pottery rates several footnotes in most archaeological studies of the subject, but for myself I could never understand why beat-up old ceramic scraps should interest anybody but professors with lots of time on their hands and no healthy outlets for their energy. (Maybe that attitude explains my never graduating from college, or why I picked up a habit instead of a Hobby; or both.)

The next gallery was visible through another arch, at right angles to the first. Even after I had looked over the floor plan of the museum, and learned to make my way around in it somehow, I never really understood why one room or corridor connected with another at just the angle and in just the direction that it indisputa-bly did. On this first visit, I didn't even try to figure it out.

The second gallery was more interesting: armour and medieval armaments, most impressive under that dull brazen light and against that wine-dark wallpaper and hangings. I kept walking, but my attention had been tweaked.

The third room, a long and narrow one, held most of the Remington cowboy scenes, and a few sculptural casts of the Dying Gladiator school. For some reason, this was the darkest gallery in the whole place—you could hardly see to keep your footing; but the squeaky floor gave you a sort of sonar sense of the walls and furnishings, as if you were a bat or a dolphin or a blind man.

After that came the framed posters from World War I ("Uncle Sam Wants YOU!") and the 19th century stage placards, well lit by individual lamps attached to their frames, though some of the bulbs had burned out. Next was a big, drafty central rotunda set about tastefully with cannon from Cortez' conquests and a silver gilt grand piano, decorated with Fragonard cupids, which Liszt once played, or made a girl on top of, or something.

All this time no sight of a human being, nor any sound except the creaking floorboards under my feet. I was beginning to wonder whether the museum staff only came out of the woodwork after sunset.

But when I had made my way up a sagging ebon staircase to the second floor, and poked my nose into a narrow, boxlike hallway with small, bleary windows on both sides (which I figured must be the covered drawbridge to the donjon keep I'd glimpsed from outside), I did finally hear some tentative echoes of presumably human activity. What kind of activity it was hard to say, though.

First of all, it seemed a sort of distant, echoing mumble, like a giant groaning in his sleep. Granted the peculiar acoustics here, I could put this down to someone talking to himself—not hard to imagine, if he worked in this place. Next, from ahead, I caught further creaking, coming from the annex, that was analogous to the racket I had been stirring up myself all along from those Nightingale Floors. The sound advanced and I was almost startled when the thoroughly prosaic figure responsible hove into view at the end of the corridor—startled either because he was so prosaic, or because it didn't seem right to meet any living, corporeal being in these surroundings; I couldn't figure out which.

This old fellow was staff, all right: his casual shuffle and at-home attitude proclaimed it, even if he hadn't been wearing a shiny blue uniform and cap that looked as if they'd been salvaged from some home for retired streetcar motormen.

'I saw the sign outside,' I said to the old man as he approached, without preliminaries, and rather to my own surprise. 'Do you still have that night watchman job open?'

He looked me over carefully, eyes sharply assessing in that faded, wrinkled mask of age; then motioned me silently to follow him back along the corridor to the keep and into the dilapidated, unutterably cluttered, smelly office from which, I learned, he operated as Day Custodian.

That was how I went to work for the Ehlers Museum.

III

My elderly friend, whose name was Mr. Worthington, himself comprised all the day staff there was, just as I constituted the entire night staff. A pair of cleaning ladies came in three days a week to wage an unsuccessful war against dust and mildew, and a furnace man shared the night watch in winter; that was all. There was no longer a curator in residence, and the board of directors (all busy elderly men with little time to spend on the museum) were already seeking new homes for the collections, anticipating the rumored demolition of the neighbourhood.

In effect, the place was almost closed now, though an occasional serious specialist or twittery ladies' club group came through; like as not rubbing shoulders with snot-nosed slum school kids on an outing, or some derelict drunk come in to get out of the cold, or heat.

Worthington told me all this, and also the salary for the night job, which wasn't high because they had established the custom of hiring university students. I made a rapid mental calculation and determined that this amount would feed me, while my quarterly annuity payments went mostly to the monkey. So I told Worth-ington yes. He said something about references and bonding, but somehow we never actually got around to that.

I was relieved to learn that, since the public was not admitted during the twelve hours I was on duty, I would not be expected to wear one of the rusty uniforms.

I asked Worthington about the founder, but the old man hadn't been on the staff long enough to remember Frederick Elhers in person, who was rumored to be quite an eccentric. The Ehlers money had come from manipulation of stocks and bonds before the turn of the century, and most of his later years were spent travelling to build up the collections, which had become his only interest in life.

Now, the rest of my story is where the plausibility gap, as they say nowadays, comes in. I've already told you I was a junkie in those days, so you can assume if you please that whatever I say happened from then on was simply hallucination. And I can't claim with any assurance or proof that you're not right.

Against that, put the fact that my habit was a very moderate one, and I was a gingerly, cautious, unconvinced sort of dope-taker. I shot just enough of the stuff to keep cheerful, if you know what I mean: dope picked me up, made the world look implausibly bright and optimistic; but not enough to give me any visions or ecstatic trances, which I wasn't looking for anyway. I was always a reality man, strange as that may sound coming from me. Only once in a while reality got a bit too abrasive, and the need arose to lubricate the outer surfaces in contact with my personality, by means of a little of that soothing white powder. Dope was my escape, like TV or booze or women serve with others.

The moderation of my habit enabled me to kick it cold turkey on my own after I left the museum job. But that's another story.

Very well, then: before I started this night watchman job (and for that matter afterwards) I had never had any experiences with far-out fancies or waking nightmares or sensory aberrations. All during the time I worked there (it wasn't long) I did have such experiences. Either that, or the things really happened that I thought were happening.

You be the judge.

IV

It started my very first night on the job. I checked in at six p.m., by which time Worthington had had an hour since closing time to batten down the hatches and lock up. He was to turn the keys over to me, and I would lock the big, ornate door, as broad as a raft, behind him. From that time I was on my own until he came back at six a.m. I could make the rounds when, as and if I saw fit; or simply doze, read, or cut out paper dolls.

I had asked old Worthington about the incidence of trouble at night, and he answered that there wasn't much.

I mentioned the j.d. gangs that could be expected in such a neighborhood, but he insisted there was hardly any difficulty with kids, except sometimes around Hallowe'en, when the smaller ones might dare each other to try to break in through the windows on the lower floors. That wouldn't be for a while yet. Anyway, I was all fitted out with a .45, a nightstick, and a powerful flash, and the precinct police station was only a block or so away. Accordingly, I anticipated a boring stint, so started from the first shooting my daily ration of junk just before coming on duty, to keep my thinking positive. It crossed my mind once or twice that this was a pretty spooky place to hang out in overnight, but I was a rationalist then, with no discernible superstitions, and thus didn't dwell on the idea.

The first evening when I came on, feeling no pain, it was already almost dark. Worthington left me with a few casual words of admonition, and I and my monkey were alone in the shadowy museum.

The lights in the entry hall were always kept on, plus the ones in the second floor office across the way in the keep; and of course there were night lights at set intervals, though they didn't do much to relieve the gloom. Especially in that badly-lit gallery of Wild West art you couldn't see your hand in front of your face, and I always had to use the flash.

The first time I made the rounds took me more than an hour, since I stopped to look over any exhibits that attracted my attention. As I passed the cases of stuffed alligators, Etruscan jewelry, and Civil War battle flags, I found myself wondering what sort of guy Frederick Ehlers could have been to devote so much of his time and fortune to such random purchases. Maybe things out of the past simply fascinated him, no matter what they were, the way they do some kids and professional historians.

By the time I ended up in the keep, it was pitch dark outside.

I'd noticed as I sauntered along that those musical floorboards sounded twice as loud at night as they did in the daytime, and reflected that this made it virtually impossible for a thief or prowler to escape detection—and also impossible for me to sneak up on any such intruder. The place had two-way, built-in radar.

I spent maybe half an hour in the keep, flashing my light over a really fascinating array of medieval artifacts, including some of those ingenious torture instruments that seem so to obsess the modern mind. This gallery was arranged a little more logically than most of the displays, and held the interest better.

As I was starting back across the drawbridge-like corridor, I noticed that my footsteps as magnified by the squeaky flooring seemed to echo back at me from ahead even louder than I had noticed on the way over. Alerted by the narcotic I had taken, my subconscious must have noticed some inconsistency of rhythm or phasing in that echoed sound, for I found myself, for no discernible reason, stopping stock still.

From far ahead, the rhythmic squeaking continued!

Sweat popped out on me, though the evening was chilly. An intruder? Or had old Worthington returned? But he surely would have hailed me to avoid being shot at, in case I turned out to be a trigger-happy type. No, it must be a prowler, someone who had either broken in or secreted himself before the museum closed.

I broke into a trot, heedless of noise, since stealth was impossible anyway. Once across the drawbridge, I stopped again to listen, and thought I had gained on the sound, which seemed to be coming from below. I fumbled my way down the stairs to the first floor and dashed ahead, using my flash discreetly where needed. As I paused outside the pitch-dark Remington gallery, I realized the sound was coming from just inside.

I plunged into the gallery and swept my flash over the wine-red draperies, over the Indian paintings and bronzes of horses and cowboys. My ears told me the creaking was now at the opposite side of the narrow room and moving toward the arched exit. I ran on, directing the light through the archway; then, once more involuntarily, I halted.

The squeaking of the floor progressed deliberately past the exit and into the gallery beyond, but my light revealed nothing visible to cause the sound!

Now the sweat that had broken out on my body turned cold.

Suddenly, the sound ceased entirely; but even as I moved forward to investigate, I heard it start again upstairs.

Doggedly, I turned in my tracks, re-crossed the dark gallery, and puffed my way back up the stairs.

The creaking now seemed diffused, echoing from a dozen ambiguous sources—as fast as I would track one down, it would evaporate and others cut in, some upstairs others again below.

Finally my uncanny sensation dissolved before the ludicrousness of the situation. Here I was chasing noises all over a haunted house, stirring up more echoes with my clumsy footfalls than I could ever succeed in running down. I leaned against a display case, winded, and laughed out loud. As I did so, the crackling and creaking noises all over the building reached a peak, dwindled, and gradually ceased.

I began to consider what might have caused this disconcerting visitation. The most logical answer was probably the cooling and shrinkage of the floorboards in the chilly night air. This could occur in random patterns of self-activating sound. Added to this, perhaps, might be the factor of my own weight traversing the floor, depressing certain boards which, as they cooled and shrank, sprang back in sequence, creating the effect of ghostly footsteps.

Still in a moderate state of euphoria, I convinced myself that this was certainly the case, and began to feel ashamed of my initial panicky reactions.

I went back to the little office, brewed some coffee on the hot-plate, and ate a sandwich I had brought with me. After a while, I made the rounds of the museum again, stepping lightly and gingerly, as if my care could exorcise the sinister eruption of sounds that had beset me earlier.

This time, outside of a few odd groanings and shiftings normal in an old building, there were no noises. Once in a while during the night there came brief flurries of distant squeaking, but I finally gave up attempts to locate them through sheer boredom. It was too monotonous trying to creep up and surprise a mere nervous chunk of wood suffering from hot and cold flashes.

I even napped for a while in the office toward dawn.

At six a.m., shortly after daybreak, I went down to answer Mr. Worthington's bell. As he entered, stoop-shouldered and rather pathetic in his threadbare day-shift uniform, he asked in a disinterested tone, 'All quiet?'

I wondered if he was joking. 'I wouldn't call it that, exactly,' I answered. 'The place was creaking and crackling half the night. Sounded as if all the ghost legions of Crusaders who owned that armour had come back to claim it.'

'Oh, the floors. Yes, most of our night men mention that at first. Scares some of them out of a year's growth. I forgot to tell you about it.'

I stared at Mr. Worthington's inoffensive form with a feeling of fierce contempt I hope my expression concealed. The warmth of my reaction surprised me; I must have been more rattled last night than I realized.

I went home and went to bed

V

Well, like the other night men at the museum, I got used to the noise after a while. (Or maybe they didn't; maybe that was why the job was open so often.) After all, I was on an especially potent kind of tranquilliser. The work was easy, the pay and the hours were steady, and I had no kicks—outside of the kind I sought myself at the tip of a needle.

I wasn't getting anywhere; but, as I've intimated, I was never sure just where it was I might want to get anyway.

The second phase of the business started when I commenced to see things as well as hear them. *Almost* to see things, that is, which was the maddening part of it. Actually I would never catch a straight glimpse of anything odd: just flickers out of the corner of my eye, a fugitive flurry of barely-sensed movement that disappeared no matter how quickly I turned to confront it; furtive shiftings in the mass of solid objects as I passed by. It's not an experience I can describe very clearly, nor one that I would wish to repeat.

This kind of visual impression might or might not be synchronized with the creaking of the floors, nearby or distant. The coinciding of the two phenomena occurred so much at random, in fact, that I somehow sensed there was no connection, at least no causative connection, between them.

I wondered whether Old Man Ehlers had seen and heard things here too, and whether that might have had anything to do with his being found dead of a heart attack in the medieval gallery one morning during the winter of 1927, as Mr. Worthington had told me.

Now I really began to get concerned. Other people had heard the noises, or so I'd been told, and there were conceivable natural explanations for them. But nobody at the museum, as far as I knew, had ever mentioned seeing things, and I couldn't bring myself to mention the matter to old Worthington. I wasn't yearning for a padded cell, or Lewisburg, at this juncture.

I drew the natural conclusion and knocked off on dope for a few days. But it made no difference, except then I was so nervous and shaky that my delusions (if that's what they were) might have been withdrawal symptoms as easily as narcotic hallucinations. They had me, coming and going.

It was about this time that I found Old Man Ehlers' journal.

VI

You see, these delusions of sound and sight, whatever they were, didn't afflict me all the time. (That would have sent me starko, despite my alleged skepticism.) They went on for maybe ten or fifteen minutes once or twice or even half a dozen times a night; there was never any way to predict. The rest of the time I used to occupy with reading, to fill up the gaps between my increasingly infrequent rounds.

This particular night I'd forgotten to bring a book, so I

rummaged around the cluttered office in the keep for something to browse through while I consumed my sandwich and coffee.

I located some moldy old volumes sagging abandoned in a decrepit breakfront pushed back in one corner; they seemed mostly antiquarian guides, but my eye fell on a thin book with no title on the spine. I pulled it out and discovered it was a daily journal, dated 1925 and stamped with the name Frederick Ehlers. It was dusty enough that it might not have been opened in the thirty-odd years since Ehlers died, but I cleaned it up a bit and began to page through it.

At first I was disappointed, although the human fascination with sticking one's nose into someone else's private business kept me reading.

It was neither a diary nor a business journal, but seemed to consist mostly of accounts of dreams the old boy had had, plus speculations on their meaning, with occasionally a few rather visionary philosophical jottings thrown in.

Some of the dreams were dillies. I remember one that went something like this: "Dreamed I was shut inside the new Iron Maiden from Dusseldorf. A noisy crowd outside was laughing, jeering, and hammering on it; and gradually it became red hot. Feeling of terror, not at the pain, but because I was certain those outside were *not human.* Meaning: birth trauma, or perhaps some ritual of spiritual purification?"

There was a lot of stuff like that, not very reassuring as to the inner psychic life of Our Founder, and I had begun to tire of deciphering the jagged, fading ink strokes, when suddenly an extended passage caught my attention. I copied it down and still have it, so I can quote it accurately:

"That objects with a long history, particularly those associated with passionate or violent people and events, soak up and retain an aura or atmosphere of their own I have no doubt. And that under certain conditions they may produce a tangible emanation, even sensory stimuli, is proved by my experiences as a collector. Perhaps one must be psychic, whatever that may mean, to receive these impressions, which would explain why not all collectors have had such experiences.

"I don't mean only manifestations like the squeaking of the ancient floorboards I brought over and installed from the wrecked Daimyo's mansion after the Tokyo earthquake (though that is an especially unnerving instance), but also certain definite sights and emotional impressions, sounds, odours, etc. How otherwise explain the smell of blood, the feeling of horror surrounding most ancient torture instruments? It cannot be association, since the effects are felt even when the objects are hidden and unsuspected by the subjects in tests I have made.

"These phenomena, of course, are not 'ghosts' in any literal or personal sense, but more like the recordings impressed on a phonographic cylinder. Still, since I am unsure whether or not such emanations can affect matter physically, there is a chance they may be more powerful, and perhaps dangerous, than mere recordings could be."

That was all; next came another crazy dream, and nothing else in the book continued this train of thought, although there were some weird, rather theosophical speculations on spiritual life inhabiting inorganic matter.

Still, it meant that the man who had originally assembled this jumble-sale collection had himself heard, seen, and felt things here that he couldn't explain, except through this fanciful theorising, over thirty years ago. And my guess about the Japanese origin of the Nightingale Floors was correct—an almost fantastic coincidence! (Could I myself perhaps be "psychic, whatever that may mean"?) I began to feel closer to, and sorrier for, that lonely, visionary millionaire who bequeathed this house of horrors to an indifferent community.

Suddenly, faint in the distance, I heard the muffled sound of a piano playing. It was not a radio, not a recording, but unmistakably an echo from the drafty rotunda downstairs where reposed the fragile, ornate instrument once reputedly owned by Liszt.

I walked downstairs as if in a dream, hardly aware of what I was doing. I knew the piece: it was Liszt's *Campanella*; someone played it in a Hitchcock movie once, and it had stuck in my mind: fragile, elfin bells in a silver tintinnabulation of sound. As I entered the lofty rotunda the piano, deep in shadow, loomed across the room, stark Spanish cannon silhouetted incongruously against it as still deeper shadows.

My eyes adjusted to the gloom and began to half-discern what appeared to be a dark, swaying, undefined shape hovering above the keyboard, moving in the circumscribed patterns a rapt player might follow. The music still had a distant, stifled quality, and I wondered if the ancient hammers and pedals were really moving: surely the instrument would not be in tune after so many years. But what had Ehlers written? "Objects... associated with passionate people and events soak up and retain an aura, and may produce a tangible emanation, even sensory stimuli..."

Suddenly the racket of the Nightingale Floors erupted around me again, louder than ever before, deafening, from all over the house, so that the spell holding me broke and I felt terror, bewilderment; and turned to run, to flee this strange museum with its entombed but living sampling of the past.

But the only way out lay through the unlit Remington gallery, that tomb-black trap I had always distrusted. And I had left both flashlight and weapons upstairs!

There was no other choice, and as I blundered into the room of Wild West art I sensed that it was neither entirely dark nor entirely untenanted.

Outlined in a light that was not light, since it did not diffuse, I saw the erect, majestic form of an Indian chief in full ceremonial regalia: feathered headdress, buckskin leggings, beaded belt, with a crude bow slung across one bare, muscular shoulder. (Could an artist's intensification of reality also entrap an image from the past, even though the painting itself had never been in the physical presence of its subject?)

The figure of the Indian moved lithely toward the centre of the chamber, but I was past it already, bounding through the archway opposite as if propelled by the crackling of the floors, now intensified to such a degree that it resembled a fireworks display.

I staggered into the next gallery, but stopped short to locate and avoid any further unnatural phenomena there.

This was one of the medieval rooms, and at first it seemed there was nothing unusual here except the frantic snapping of the flooring. Then my glance fell on an Elizabethan headsman's axe mounted on the wall, faintly illuminated by one of the dim night lights several yards distant.

Before my eyes, a wavering form shaped itself around the axe, stabilized, and came clear, lifelike: the black-hooded, swarthy figure of the executioner, both brawny fists grasping the haft of the immense, double-headed weapon, which hung at an angle as if to accommodate itself to the natural grip of the burly beadsman.

I wheeled in panic and sprinted for the front door, threw back the night latch, and half-stumbled down the stairs and across the mangy lawn under the spectral benches of the great poplars, whose dry leaves rattled and chattered as if in derisive echo of the tumultuous uproar of the floorboards in the empty building behind me.

I phoned in my resignation to Mr. Worthington next day (since, superstitious as my attitude might seem, I never wished to enter the Ehlers Museum again) and started the long comeback path to a normality in which I could at least distinguish between the real and the illusory. Which is about all any of us can claim, at best.

For I had seen something during those last few seconds in the museum that frightened me more than anything else I experienced that night.

I have said that the apparition of a giant executioner gripping his axe had appeared in the medieval gallery. Well, the axe was mounted on the wall just above another quaint relic of those earlier days when our savagery was less subtle: the rough-hewn wooden headsman's block.

And as the figure of the executioner coalesced around his axe, so another figure—supine, hands bound, neck wedged in the gruesomely functional V-shaped depression—materialized around the block.

The face was turned toward me, and I recognized from photos the florid, mutton-chopped visage of Frederick Ehlers, long-dead founder of the museum, staring in terror—still caught in his endless chain of nightmares, still a prisoner (but now a part) of those "tangible emanations" from the past which he had painstakingly assembled and which he had finally and forever, inescapably joined.

THE PREVIOUS TENANT

By Ramsey Campbell

H E CLOSED THE CUPBOARD door and crossed to the window. The pane exhibited ghostly strokes of soap, like the paint sketched on the sheet of paper he'd crumpled up last week. In the next room his wife moved a table, which screamed. He stared out. The roofs were a jagged frieze against the colours spilled to mix on the horizon; below, the red streetlamps tasted of raspberry, tinting the trees like attenuated pine-cones separated by the ruler of the pavement. A car passed, hushed as the evening, casting ahead on the road what seemed already a splash of yellow paint. It wasn't enough for him to express on canvas. He turned back to the flat room, the wallpaper's pastel leaves whose meaning had been lost through countless prints, the bed he must never touch without having bathed. He had remembered what he'd seen as the cupboard door had closed.

The imprisoned books rebuked him; already, on the Renoir, a coil of dust curled and fidgeted like a centipede. What he'd seen was crushed beneath Matisse and Toulouse-Lautrec; he hoisted them and slid it out. It was a photograph of the girl who had owned the flat: one leg high on a wall, her skirt taut, her hand arched on her knee, her eyes beneath an arch of lustrous hair smiling at whoever held the camera; how could she have become a scream above the city, a broken figurine beneath the window? His wife coughed. At once he thrust the photograph into his pocket. At the door he turned to check the cupboard. It was closed.

His wife was cross-legged on the carpet, surrounded by the glasses from the cabinet, considering the space available. 'I've done the best I can,' he said.

She dabbed a bead of lacquer from her forehead. 'It's not your books I object to, you know that,' she told him... it's just that there's not enough space, that's all.'

'I don't remember you complaining when we looked it over.'

'Who'd complain at a flatful of furniture?' Above her stood the antique chairs, the glass-topped tables, the mirrors with which the girl had surrounded herself. 'But there's such a thing as being over-generous, you know.'

He was silent; he didn't want to say 'we should be grateful.'

'If we get rid of a few of these things you could have your painting on the wall.'

'There's no point.' Not in one painting and a hundred crumpled scraps of drawing-paper.

'It might brighten the place up a little.'

'That's a profound analysis,' He watched her stretch her legs, hemmed in by the glasses; it seemed a perfect symbol—he would have transferred it to canvas if he had been able to paint her.

'I know I don't have your intellect.' She picked up a glass; in a club she wouldn't long have held it empty.

'I've never said so, have I? What you don't have is sensitivity to this flat. It's the girl's life. There's the chair where she must have sat when she composed the note. Or is that what's bothering you?'

'It doesn't bother me at all, you know that. I'm not the one who lies awake.' She spread a cloth on the table and filled two glasses. 'Just a few things of my own, that's all I ask. I don't like charity.'

And the men at the ballroom? What did she call the drinks they bought her at their clubs? 'You're not in all that much,' he said.

'It's not my fault if you won't come with me.'

'Can't afford to come with you, you mean.' His words thrust like a tongue toward an aching tooth. His fingers traced his inside pocket, the photograph symmetrical with his heart.

'Don't, don't. You're hurting yourself.' She carried a glass to him.

24

As he took it, she laid her hand on his within the concealed rectangle. 'You can't be both a civil servant and a painter. Don't try for so much or you'll lose everything,' she said. 'Let's leave the flat to look after itself for tonight. Our room is ours.'

'Do hurry,' she said, 'I'm so tired.' Deflated, he lay back. In a minute the moonlit sheet over her breasts was rising and falling like surf. He inched to sit up. His side of the bed was a scribble of shadow like paint scrawled in fury. Perhaps this might be meaningful on canvas. *Bedroom Scene, The Marriage Bed*—but he couldn't express their marriage. She had been a civil service typist; as she'd passed him, glanced and smiled, his pen had come erect between his fingers; the next time she passed he had sketched the memory. When she came to look he'd said 'I'd like to paint you.' 'That would be nice,' she'd replied, 'but not nude.' Baulked, for she had destroyed his dream, he'd postponed the offer through months of clumsy dancing in ballrooms where smoke billowed to meet clouds of false stars, of hands across club tables at one in the morning; seeking to possess her, he'd foregone the rushing skies, the stretched clouds, the combed and recombed grass, which met at his easel and poured into his brush, and he'd suffocated. When they emerged from the cramped registrar's he'd found he couldn't paint. On the wedding night she'd cried out; briefly he'd possessed her. Yet before the honeymoon was over he'd yearned for something more; he'd gazed from the hotel at rumpled trees, humped hillside walls where the girl from the photograph might have stood and smiled. 'Don't forget to give in your notice,' he'd reminded his wife. 'I'll keep you.' Perhaps thus he could possess her. But his walks possessed the breasts of the hills, the splayed thighs of the valleys. Then one night he'd been whipped home by a storm and had found her gone. An hour later she'd slammed the front door, gasping happily, thrilled by the leaping rain, and had halted at the sight of him sunk deep in a dark chair. She'd stroked his hair; rain coursed down their merged faces like tears. They'd gone upstairs to find the house was cracked; rain dripped somewhere. They couldn't afford the repairs, and at last they'd agreed before a landlord's card bulged and distorted by the trembling globes of a new rain: this flat, close to the country as she'd said, closer to the raw red sign of the ballroom round the corner as he'd thought. He slid down the bed to mould himself to her, but she was still asleep. He turned over. The moonlight fell short of the wardrobe, where his suit hid the photograph. The cupboard of books was held within skins of sleep which weighed on his eyes; next to it, his easel was a dusty blackboard. As he drowsed into sleep, he thought the cupboard opened.

'Wear your nice suit today,' she said. 'I like to see you in it.'

'All right, for you.' The sunlight slid from cars and coated leaves with light; it might become a painting. He collected pens and wallet from the table by the bed and followed her into the living-room. As he entered she drew the table-cloth across a brilliant sheet of pressed sunlight and pinned it down with bowls of cereal; through the sheet he'd seen its carved legs, shaped as by caresses. 'If you think we can't afford furniture,' she mused, 'I could always go back to work.'

'I don't think that's called for.' Shaped as by caresses. His hand stole beneath the cloth and touched the wood. Slowly, exquisitely, his fingers traced the curves. He saw the leg braced on the wall, the taut skirt. His wife picked up her spoon; it blazed at the edge of his eye. Unlacquered, her hair glowed. Suddenly ashamed, he reached out and stroked her knee.

'Not when you're eating, please,' she said. 'Your hands are greasy.'

At the door he realized that he couldn't go back for the photograph; if he did his wife would know. Instead, he looked up at the

26

window through the leaves piled like her hair. The pane was white as an empty canvas; within, a figure shielded her eyes and waved.

When he came home that night his mind was covered with sketches, erased lines, sheets half-torn and reassembled with conjecture. He'd imagined the tree-lined street washed by head-lamps as the girl had seen it, staring down, perhaps for a last glimpse of whoever had abandoned her—the unknown hand on the camera shutter no longer holding hers. In the lunch-hour he'd sketched on the back of a form, but the sketch had lacked a sight of the reality. 'Don't lay the table yet,' he told his wife as he veered into the kitchen, 'I have an idea I want to get down.' The people in the flat below were across the city when the girl had screamed and fallen, but they were sure that she had been abandoned; a drained husk, perhaps she'd thought that she might float toward the empty landscape. He set up his easel before the window. The room seemed more cramped than he remembered; he would have to sit on the bed. He projected the girl on the pane, but she refused to pose; her foot poised on the sill, the weighted falling sun shone through her skirt. That wasn't what he wanted. Already the street-lamps were raw wounds on the night; a tree shed a leaf like a flake of skin. If he could see her perhaps he would be able to persuade her to pose. He crossed to the wardrobe and felt in the pocket for the photograph. There was no pocket. The suit was gone.

You did that on purpose, said his nails biting into the wood. The sun sank and touched the black horizon. He tramped into the kitchen. 'So you got rid of my suit,' he said.

'You don't think I wouldn't ask you first?' Behind her head a curtain swayed like a skirt. 'It's only at the cleaner's. You're an artist—I'd have thought you'd care how you looked.'

'So that I'll get on, I know. I didn't think you'd go behind my back.'

'If there was anything in it you wanted I'm sorry, honestly I am.

I couldn't find anything.'

'Nothing I haven't already got.'

'This table really is too small, you know,' she said. The cruet came down hard on the clothed glass. She knows! it exclaimed. Or had she fumbled it rather than thumped it down as a protest? No, he was sure she had the photograph. She withdrew herself from him by sleeping, then she stole his souvenir. The carved leg pressed his. 'I like the flat as it stands,' he told her. 'It welcomes me.'

As he stood before the cupboard plates chattered in the kitchen. No doubt the girl had washed up for her lover; perhaps they'd eaten at two in the morning, their hours based on their shared rhythm, not imposed from outside—the sort of life he meant when he yearned to be bohemian. Arms about each other, they'd tire together when at all. He opened the cupboard door; he would find a book which might suggest a detail to extend across his empty canvas. In the shadows the titles were dim. He knew each by its place. He touched the tip of a spine, and a finger flattened beneath his own.

He wasn't menaced; he didn't recoil. Instead he reached up and brought the glove to his face. It glimmered white on his palm. The fingers were stiff, perhaps starched. He held it by the knuckles and let the fingers rest arched on his hand.

In the kitchen a knife scraped. His wife had finished. Carefully be laid the glove over the books, where it posed lightly, coquettishly. He closed the door softly, as if apologetic, and returned to the easel. In a moment the girl in the photograph might move as desired and stare from the window. But the sun's last shards were blunted; at a crossroads in the centre of the landscape, traffic-lights tripped up and down their scale. Two glasses chimed. He cursed his wife; jealous, she'd driven away his model. He strode out of the bedroom. 'Are you going out?' he demanded.

She arranged the first ring of glasses, encircling the table-leg. 'I want to do as much as I can tonight,' she said. 'Anyway, I thought you might like me to stay in.'

'When I'm painting?' She turned to him: surely he could have left that unsaid. 'Watch what you're doing!' he shouted, but too late; kneeling, she overbalanced and her hand, flinching away from the glasses, caught the table-leg. The table reared. The glass top came down on the arm of a chair, and a star flew out between them.

'Oh, I am sorry,' she cried, on the edge of tears. 'I didn't mean to.' But he'd rushed to the table and grasped a carved leg. The ruined top ground and splintered and he whirled, brandishing the leg, topped with a head of jagged glass like an axe.

'I didn't do it on purpose. I wouldn't have done that.' She tried to catch hold of his hand as it drooped. 'We'd better get rid of it before someone gets hurt,' she said.

'Throw away the glass but leave the legs. I may be able to use them sometime. In a carving,' he added bitterly.

In the night he sat up. His wife's face lay upward on the pillow, helpless. The black sun was hot beneath the horizon, like a coal about to set fire to the air. He plodded through the flat and turned on the kitchen light. The carved legs were piled in a corner; above them an edge of the curtain swayed. He thought he heard his wife call out. He would fight her; he would complete a painting to express the flat. If only he could see the girl, find the photograph. Behind him the door banged and sprang back. Someone moved silently to stand behind him, her hands almost touching his shoulders. She didn't tint the white tiles of the kitchen. He swung about. Only the restless door moved. 'I wouldn't have left you,' he said almost to himself.

His wife was propped up by the pillows, waiting. 'What were you doing?' she asked.

'There was something I wanted from the kitchen. I didn't

expect to find you awake.'

'There's a rat in your cupboard,' she said.

'Nonsense. What would a rat want in there?'

'I heard something scratching at the door. If you're not going to look, I will.'

She slid out and was round the bed before he could move. Aghast, he slapped the light-switch. Electric light thrust out the moonbeams. She pulled open the door and craning on tiptoe, leaned her head inside. At last she decided: 'It must be in the wall.'

As she returned to bed he extinguished the light. 'You haven't closed the cupboard properly,' he said. He opened the door as if to shut it with a slam. A moonbeam partitioned him off from the bed. He laid his hand on the rim of the cupboard, waiting, and the glove fell on his fingers like a caress.

Dear Sir, I am in receipt of your letter—On the back he sketched the glove. At once his pencil traced her poised arm and ranged over her curves, the lead point sensitive as his fingertips. It smoothed her hair and formed the framed oval. But her face eluded him. The shutter of his mind had jammed. Was she facing him or smiling secretly in profile? He drove the point into the paper close to her hair, and the pencil snapped.

'We'll have to eat in here tonight,' said his wife from the kitchen. 'I know it's crowded.'

He threw his overcoat on the bed; he should have an overall to welcome him, a vortex of colour like petrol after rain.

She was wearing a grey sweater; she looked young as a rediscovered photograph. Opened, the oven door exhaled the heavy heat of steak. She encircled the meat with potatoes and smiled. 'When I was dusting your books—'

His knife froze in the meat. 'You were dusting my books?'

'I thought it was the least I could do. I found a glove. I thought

30

at first it was the rat.'

And he'd torn up the sketched hand. 'What have you done with it?' The knife gouged; the meat tore.

'I threw it away, of course. It would have ruined your books. It was covered with—I don't know, it was all wet.'

'With tears, perhaps. No, no, it doesn't matter.'

The pillow gasped as his fist drove in. The bedroom was void. He left his easel in the corner. Already the girl's presence had attenuated; she'd begun to fray, to be absorbed into the flat like mist. Or to drift out of the window; his wife was systematically driving her out, destroying the expressions of her personality, his tokens of her. Clouds bulged from the lacklustre sky like wet wallpaper. He stared at the unlined sheets, willing even the curve of her leg to form. One sight of her face and he would possess her. But he felt sure the photograph was ashes. Suddenly he caught up his easel and bore it toward the window. There would be a suspended silent moment before the easel smashed and scattered on the concrete. He thrust the window high. A breeze breathed into his eyes, and for a second a cloud smiled beneath hair. At once he knew. With gestures sure as sketched lines he set up the easel. Then patiently he lay back on the bed to wait.

He leapt up. His wife was sorting plates and cutlery on the kitchen table. 'I won't be in your way,' she said. 'I won't be, will I?'

Without a word he clutched the carved legs and returned to the bedroom. Each leg was wood. Unprepared for the end of a curve, his fingers constantly fell into space. He laid one leg against his; when he moved the edge cut into his flesh. The wood was lifeless. The cupboard was empty. One side of the canvas had slipped low; a corner encroached on the wide dull landscape. The girl was elsewhere. Even the touch of the glove had been too light to suggest so much as the ghost of a hand. Abandoned once, she would never return again if re-buffed. And yet, he thought—and yet his painting might provide her with a hold. She might become the painting.

Light resonated in the glasses like a soundless chime. He stood before the kitchen door; his throat was dry. The kitchen was her last refuge. Surely it contained nothing that his wife might shatter. The girl knew this as surely as he did. Yet he was afraid to enter; it would be their first meeting. And his wife would be alert.

The door swung in his wake. She came to meet him. Yet not quite; her presence was lent a harsh immediacy by the white tiles, compressed by the pendulous sky, but not formed. She was still preparing for him. He must wait. As he whirled, impatient, he glimpsed his wife's face, flat as a painting against the wall.

He paced the bedroom. The sky was close as the walls, encasing his eyes. He found that he could hear himself breathing, almost suffocated. He wrenched open the cupboard door and dragged out a sketch-pad. A title for his painting. Anything. But the edges of the pencil were insufferable as the angles of a rusty threepence. A book to calm him. The art-paper scraped beneath his nails, agonizing as tin. He dropped the book and rushed into the kitchen.

'Oh, what is it?' his wife cried. 'Don't keep going away from me!'

At the sound of her voice the girl fled. The kitchen rejected her. He stared slowly at his wife, the neat ranks of cutlery, the hand-kerchief bulging the arm of her sweater like a muscle. 'God. God. God,' he said.

And then he fell silent.

Behind her head, like an embryo born of the breeze, the curtain swelled. A thrust of air created cheekbones from its folds. Above them hollows might harbour whatever expression he called forth. The line which linked the hollows fell away into an arch. As the curtain swayed a wrinkle smiled, but shyly.

His wife followed the line of his gaze. 'Oh, the curtain,' she said. 'Why didn't you say it was crumpled?'

She shook it straight. For a moment it was sucked against the

32

window-frame, as if clutched in panic and relinquished. The tips of a tree were veiled, then sprang bright.

The table shook at his clutch. 'Won't come back,' he muttered.

'Sorry?' But his face was frozen as a portrait. 'You look so lost tonight,' his wife said. 'Can I give you something?'

The planes of the kitchen were flat as the untinted tiles. He would never know what colour of dress the girl had worn; nor that only skulls lack a nose. He peered through a wavering mist at the table. His hand closed on a carving-knife. 'This'll do,' he said.

THE NIGHT FISHERMAN

By Martin I. Ricketts

NIGHT FISHING. There was nothing quite like it. There was nothing quite like sitting in the darkness at the edge of a black lake, torch in hand, and watching the luminous tip of the float on the dark surface of the water. Nothing like the thrill of watching the tiny tip flip with a sudden motion before vanishing beneath the surface with a tiny "pop!" as the carp took the bait. Nothing like striking, heaving the rod sideways with a swish, and feeling the sudden fighting weight, invisible, on the other end.

Albert Jordan loved to fish at night. By day he'd tried fast-running streams and meandering rivers, but, as far as he was concerned, there was something special, something strangely fascinating about the bright tip of a plastic float on the slack, black waters of a night lake. No one else of his acquaintance could quite understand this fascination; every one of his angling friends derived their pleasure from sitting at the edge of a green swim, gently touched by the bright daylight sun, with a soft tumble of bird-song in the background, and the faint hoot of a water-fowl (faint for distance, so as not to disturb the waters of an angler's swim, of course!) hanging on the warm air. Albert, in turn, could never sympathize with *this* attitude. To him the pleasure of being alone at night at the water's silent edge was a wonderful thing, something to be worshipped with an almost religious fervour. In short, night fishing was his idea of the ultimate in pleasure.

It was in anticipation of this pleasure that Albert smiled to himself as he walked across the fields late on one particular evening. Midnight was approaching and the night was black as a cavern; all day the sky had been overcast, and now neither moon nor stars broke through the complete darkness. His gum-booted feet swishing heavily through the dew-laden grass, Albert Jordan headed in the direction of the invisible line of trees which marked the water's edge, the narrow beam of light from his torch probing faintly ahead of him, lighting the way for his feet. Hanging down from his shoulders, his basket and rod-bag bumped and rubbed against his raincoated back as he walked.

Soon he was among the trees and he half-walked, half-slid down the bank, one hand on the wet ground for support. And then the ground was horizontal once more as he found himself standing in pitch-blackness on a shelf of baked, tramped mud right at the water's edge, on which, with relief, he dropped his heavy tackle. Not a sound, not a motion besides his own, disturbed the complete darkness. He opened his basket, unfolded his canvas stool, and with experienced hands he began to tackle-up, needing no light to aid him.

At last he was ready. With an expert motion he cast, the bait falling with a quiet splash in the darkness. The float bobbed as if waving to him, moving slowly up and down a few times, and was then still, the luminous tip like an eye in the blackness in front of him. Albert sat on the stool to wait.

Minutes passed. The darkness, except for the tip of the float, was complete. Everything was still and silent.

Albert waited, warm with the knowledge of his own patience. For a long while he didn't move, he sat as if frozen, his gaze intent on the tip of the float in front of him.

Presently a soft gentle breeze, like a shiver, sprang up quickly and was gone in a second; the only sign of its passing was the brief hiss and rattle of invisible reeds somewhere nearby.

More minutes passed. Still the tiny dot floating in front of him did not move. And neither did anything else.

Soon Albert began to fidget. His fingers twitched. He swallowed. After awhile the realization dawned on him that the pleasure he had anticipated for tonight was missing. For no reason he picked up his rod and reeled in the line. With his fingertips he checked that the lobworm was still securely on the hook, and then he re-cast. The float bobbed again, silently on the black water, and was then still.

The silence and the darkness were once again filled with an intensity which crept like a ghost around him. The whole world seemed to be silently shrouded in a black, invisible cloak.

Albert suddenly realized he was nervous. Now why, he asked himself, should that be? He had never been at all afraid of the dark in his entire life. What was wrong tonight?

The stillness. That's what it was; that *must* be what it was. Never before had he been out on a night which was so dark and so completely still. Even the usual tiny watery sounds of the fish rising for food were missing.

He shivered. The blankness of such a night tended to inspire one's imagination to invent all kinds of weird and horrible things; he'd be well advised to occupy his mind with thoughts of familiar things, keeping outside of his immediate awareness the unnatural stillness of this incredibly dark night.

He began to concentrate on his fishing rod. He reached down, feeling the reassuringly familiar shape of its handle with his fingertips. The rod. It was comprised of three sections, made of fibreglass, and had metal ferrules through which the line passed. The line. Nylon: through the ferrules of the rod and down; down to the luminous float which glowed happily in front of him, a pale dot in the blackness, and then down still farther, laden with shot, to the hook.

And, impaled on the hook, was the worm.

Albert's hands kneaded each other in his lap as he thought

about it. The worm writhing and squirming, the hook through its body; the hook sharp and barbed, preventing its escape as it wriggled in the cold black water. Albert shuddered. He could almost imagine himself as the worm, could almost feel the sharp, fiery pain of the hook as it pierced his body, and the icy coldness of the water as he struggled to escape, needles of pain lancing through his chest as the hook pulled at him...

Suddenly he laughed. What a strange notion. A worm indeed! Grinning, he returned his thoughts to his fishing. He squinted in the darkness and concentrated on the tip of his float.

There! Had it moved? No, it must have been his imagination. Still, he had plenty of patience: he'd surely have a bite before long.

With frightening suddenness, moonlight shone abruptly down through a break in the clouds. The glow touched the branches of the nearby trees and fell across the bank and the reeds. The lake was calm, the water a flat sheet of lead in the faint, eerie light. Albert looked up as a quick flitting movement touched the corner of his vision.

Bats!

He shuddered involuntarily. Horrible things! In the waxy light he watched the tiny black silhouettes weaving to and fro, up and down, singing silently through the air: umbrella shreds, black shadow-patches of night, dropping and swooping with incredibly quick, furtive motions above him.

And then the moon was gone. The cold darkness swiftly closed in again like the wings of one of those flitting creatures grown suddenly to monstrous proportions.

Albert, eyes closed, was shivering. The air was biting cold against his face and hands; yet, all over his body he could feel the sweat running down his flesh in sudden sticky streams. In his mind's eye he could still see the things which had been illuminated by that brief wan glow, a glow which, now vanished, made the night seem even blacker than before. Above him he imagined the dark shapes still whipping gently to and fro. All around him he felt he could still see the drooping foliage in which his imagination now placed numerous unseen horrors, rustling and creeping, shifting ominously nearer to where he sat, alone, in the darkness at the water's edge.

Albert trembled and clenched his teeth.

From somewhere came the tiny sound of water dripping, and then it was gone.

Alone. That was the trouble. This night was darker and more frightening than any he had known, and here he was, all alone, with his usually placid imagination working at double-speed. Well, now that he was here he'd have to put up with it. Self-control, that was what was needed. He just had to pull himself together.

He concentrated on the float, the tiny spot of luminescence that floated unmoving before him on the black surface of the water. Why the hell hadn't he had a bite yet? The float hadn't moved since he got here. How long ago was that? Three hours? Ten minutes? He couldn't tell; time seemed to lose its meaning here at night on the lakeside.

He sat on the stool, hands in his lap, and stared at the float. But now the darkness was not quite silent: faintly, just on the edge of his hearing, came little whisperings and rustlings; as of tiny creatures stirring in the grass and the reeds. Or was it something else—something more sinister—coming closer?

The float. Concentrate on the float. Don't let your imagination play games with you. Albert's eyes stared into the blackness, yet he could still see the pictures that the brief touch of ghostly moonlight had painted: the flat water, the pointed reeds, the tiny, candle-wax leaves on the softly illuminated branches of the trees. The branches: crooked and long like reaching hands, like clawing fingers, like writhing snakes, like long worms...

Like long worms. Albert thought about the fat worm on the end of his line, squirming with the hook through it, waiting for the black shape of the fish to come looming through the dark water, the fish whose mouth would be open to engulf the worm, to suck at it; to suck out the nourishing innards and leave the skin empty and dead on the barbed hook. To suck...

Albert saw the float-tip suddenly move. Automatically he reached out for the rod, and then he froze. His mouth opened and closed, and his eyes became wide with horror. He could feel it. By God, he could *feel* it!

It was crawling over his flesh, a cold pulsing stickiness like a wet hand trying to grip him. Needles of pain were suddenly piercing his chest and an oozing dampness was all over him, as if... as if something were trying to suck at him, trying to suck out his insides...

Albert screamed once, briefly, and then be grabbed his rod. He yanked it sideways, and suddenly the feeling was gone. The sucking grip had vanished from his flesh and streams of fire were no longer surging through his chest.

Albert let go of the fishing rod and the float bobbed gently, once more down into the water, His body racked with shudders, Albert Jordan sat down on the stool and closed his eyes tightly against the darkness.

He just couldn't believe it. For a moment there he had actually thought he was the worm, the hook piercing through him, the line pulling at him as he squirmed desperately this way and that, and the fish sucking at him, trying to draw out his innards.

Albert shook his head. This couldn't go on; he'd have to pack up his tackle and leave. From now on he'd be strictly a day fisherman.

He reached down for his basket. The sooner he could leave this eerie place the better.

And then he stopped. Suddenly he could sense the mist. It was still completely dark, yet somehow, he knew it was there. The mist rising off the water, through the blackness, sifting through the reeds and creeping along and up the bank and among the trees. Albert could feel it on his hands and on his face, cold and fearful, and completely invisible in the pitch-darkness. Layers of it, rising slowly into him and over him like depths of icy water.

Suddenly the sharp pain returned, lancing through his body like a blade. He tried to reach his rod, but something prevented him from moving. Paralyzed, his eyes staring, he watched the luminous tip of his float disappear as, below the dark surface, a fish took the bait.

Panic churned in Albert's stomach as he squirmed at the sudden agony in his chest. It churned then rose, tearing up through his body, and then he let out one long, wild, terrified scream.

Once again the oozing stickiness was all over him, sucking, sucking, sucking at his innards. Cold and slimy it was now.

The pain in his chest was the hook on the end of a fishing-line, pushing its barb through him. The damp sliminess was the mouth of a fish closing over him; the rising layers and swirls of invisible mist were the depths of water in which he wriggled and twisted, trying to escape.

He leapt to his feet, but be was bent double with the pain of the hook through his body. The invisible slimy mouth sucked at him and the heaving mist rolled over him in moist, icy waves. He screamed and screamed, squirming and wriggling, the hook burning through him, the huge cold fish-mouth sucking and sucking at his insides.

He half-ran, half-tumbled forward, screaming, falling with a heavy splash into the black waters of the lake...

Albert Jordan's absence was noticed two days later. The angling equipment found abandoned at a local lakeside was identified as being his and the lake was therefore subsequently drained.

The body of the drowned man found on the bottom was positively identified as Albert Jordan. He was only just recognisable. It seemed as if his flesh was merely a bag containing the loose bones of his skeleton. His innards, strangely, were missing, as though they had been... sucked out.

SUGAR AND SPICE AND ALL THINGS NICE

By David A. Sutton

A T THIS TIME in the morning, the sun showers a blinding swirl of motes through the branches of a nearby tree which, spilling through the window, scatter about the room. It is one of those superb, warm mornings in late spring when not a breath of wind stirs outside and one sits, cosy and contented with the tingle of summer in one's nostrils. Outside, the occasional car shunts past, disturbing the air, caught hard and bright in the sun's perpetual gaze. Passersby appear infrequently, devoid of coats and ready for the heat of the afternoon. There is a kind of hazy, half-life to the scene, as though people and their attendant technology had become immured indoors waiting; this early dazzle of summer perhaps merely an hallucination, not to be trusted.

I used to sit by the window sometimes and gaze across the street watching life pass by in its lazy fashion. Watching the still, sombre houses on the opposite side of the road face the challenge of harsh daylight, their red bricks soiled with grime, windows dark, half-lidded with mesh curtains. Doors would be brown or green, gloss paint peeling here and there in an orgy of ultra-violet acceptance; gaining no suntan, but curling under an invisible wave of burning insistence.

My room was on the first floor, a flat, a hideaway, cool. Solid walls of books, a small gas fire, a tropical bamboo screen leading to the bedroom and beyond, the small kitchen. From my window I had a minor vista of the street below, the people, the traffic and the houses. An isolated world where folk would drop in unexpectedly, walk past the view and leave the stage finally past either the left or right hand window frame. Not much amazing happened on that stage, except once, just the daily life of part of a community. This microcosm settled easily upon my mind many a bright morning—I was the watcher, those out there the watched.

Not that I was bored by other things that the mere existence outside my window could hold my fascinated surveillance, but I would often be working on catalogues at the table next to the window which allowed an uninterrupted view out, down to the grey strip of road below and up into the pale sky. I would quite often cease work and dream easily, letting whatever happened to appear through the glass to settle on the retina, there to be converted by a brain that was normally imaginatively dormant into some bizarre saga of modern life. Life had for me become a solitary affair, a routine job working at home in which I saw few people for long periods at a time. My line was in indexing, a laborious business, but one in which I reveled. I suppose, in a way, the complete negativity of indexing, its alien-ness from life, made my desire to watch folk go about their daily tasks all the more important to me. The fantasy of words, words and more words, meaninglessly jumbled together (for so it seems sometimes) could suck the mind dry and leave a hollow, black space. The printed page has a certain fascination, but it is nonetheless an escape and there is a relief sometimes in climbing back to some sort of reality; one puts down the book and the world seems to snap suddenly back.

Anyhow, that's how I sat on that fateful morning, sheets of paper and manuscripts untidily scattered about my table, the type-writer buried under a mound of carbons. It was about eleven o'clock and I'd just finished a cup of welcome coffee and was staring out at what I considered to be my own small world, my "theatre" on which I would direct the actors through their dingy roles, and there, across the road, like a patch of brighter yellow on the sun-basked pavement stood a little girl. She was about six or seven years of age, with hair of an unusual silver-straw colour, fixed in plaits. She had a strangely moulded face with a protruding chin, blue eyes and a small, inscrutable mouth. A white turned up nose peeped through the surface dirt, which covered the rest of her face. She wore a pair of cheap, brown plastic sandals, and in complete incongruity to the rest of her clothing, a pair of torn, grey woollen socks, one of which fitted snugly to the knee and the other bulging round the ankle. A plain yellow cotton dress hung from her small, thin shoulders and her bare arms were pale in the sun.

The funny thing was, I don't remember her walking into my view; one minute I stood there with the empty mug in my hand and she wasn't there, and with the blink of an eye she stood across the way. No ball or skipping rope to play with and no friends chatting, she just stood there and her eyes burned into mine passionately. I looked away in surprise, suddenly caught in the act of "watcher". The unusual thing was, that from that distance she really shouldn't have been able to see me at all—the window would have appeared as dark and lifeless as those grim panes on the other side of the street. Anyway, briefly I had turned my gaze, now quickly I looked again.

But she was gone.

It was so silly of me to feel—what was it... afraid?—of those blue eyes of hers, but they held such a yearning and drilled into my brain for that minuscule moment of time. They were ineffably intense, with a cold kind of passion, and I realized in the quiet moments afterwards that I was shivering. That little girl had inexplicably become a major character in my dramas though so brief a bit part she had played, and I simply could not for the rest of that day shift her from my mind. Needless to say, it was not the last time, unfortunately, that I would see that bright yellow vision.

The following day I received a package from Stavely, a publisher friend of mine who invariably pushes work my way. It was a thick manuscript that required indexing, two weeks solid work at least, so I set to with a vengeance and had little time to view my small plenum.

However, one Thursday evening I looked up casually from the typewriter to see a sky darkening towards night. One or two stars had appeared high up and were winking on and off. The street lamps had just been switched on, and I think it was that which had caught my attention and caused me to look up. A breeze was scuttling a sheet of newspaper along the gutter and its line of direction led me to a billowing movement of yellow on the right. There stood the little girl, dainty and pretty even though dirty and wearing those tattered and mismatched boys' socks. Her weird eyes were burrowing through my retina in a supernatural fashion. I was so taken aback that I found I'd jumped back from the window, throwing my chair over, and was peering round the edge of the curtain like a criminal... I felt hot, and then cold and the hair along my arms moved, bristling like a haunted cat.

It was such an unnatural occurrence it left me a little watery at the knees and I had to sit down a while. The girl was no longer to be seen, but no sooner had I recovered my thoughts however, when the doorbell rang, a long shrill note, rattling inside my befuddled head. I went downstairs.

As I pulled the door back I tried to stifle a gasp, since standing there in the half-light was the little girl. I choked. I couldn't say anything, my mouth was dry and my tongue seemed swollen inexplicably.

'You want to come and play, Mister?' the voice inquired, a normal, girlish voice. A natural, smutty little girl in all respects except for those eyes, asking an innocent question of a stranger.

'Nnn... no... not today!' was all I could stammer back and I closed the door sharply. I dashed back upstairs and slammed the door to my flat, expecting any minute the clamour of the doorbell again. I sat and breathed deeply for several minutes, trying to fathom my seemingly acute fear of what was purely a natural, if isolated incident. A girl who merely wants someone to play with, who has no friends, who sees me from time to time at my window, always available; and only now has she plucked up the courage to reach up the tall door and press the bell which will bring me to her. My bell! Since there are three flats in the house, how did she know which of the three bells was mine?

I couldn't rid myself of my thoughtlessly bad manners to this small, frail human being, no matter how strangely cognizant she was of both my doorbell and me. Innocent as yet of the tortuous passages of the grown-up world and its madness. My sleeping hours would not let me forget either, and I was tormented by the fragmented images of a horrible nightmare...

In the dream I was looking out across the road to where the girl stood in her yellow dress and her eyes were red holes that sent rays of eerie light into the room. Her mouth opened slowly and mouthed silent words, her lips contorting into cruel shapes as she did so. The face stood wax-white and a slow wind moved her dress like gossamer... the image blurred, changed... She was now hacking at the front door with her fingers, the wood like soft, grey fungus giving way before her malefic onslaught. The face was twisted in a wide grin of horror, the chin protruding, saliva dripping from it, the eyes screwed tight into little knots of red hate. Then she broke through the door, the fungus falling away, tearing silently, plopping down in soggy lumps, spores puffing out clouding the scene in a multitude of minute stars... I lay under the bedclothes, her coarse breathing sounding louder as she ascended the stairs and entered the flat. The covers slipped away leaving me cold in the ball of black night. In the dark shone those twin orbs, soulless and evil, yet full of fear. Her arms outstretched, covered in something dark and foul. Everything bathed in an unearthly red light... the red light became bigger... bigger like a huge flame, a burning and crackling...

I lay in bed, awake now, shaking with the aftermath of the dream. The bedclothes lay in a heap on the floor, the nightlight beside my bed had burned right down until the wick, floating in a pool of wax, was flaring and sputtering. I blew it out with a groan of relief and reached for the light switch. Bathed in the friendly glow, I re-made the bed and tried to finish what was left of the night in untroubled sleep, but the picture of the girl, maniacal in her intensity to breach the door, strangely made of fungus and smothered in a universe of sparkling stars, did little to bring unconsciousness to me.

Nightmares have a habit of doing that.

By the end of the next week I had finished the index for the manuscript and had typed it up into a final draft. I had been so busy that the horrors of the dream were almost erased from conscious memory. I phoned Stavely and told him the thing would be with him in a day or two, which he greeted with delight, so that as I replaced the receiver I felt quite elated. The sun glowed outside, everything was right with the world, the murmur of contentment was there, and soon a big fat cheque would be on its way, doing no end of good to my failing bank balance.

I decided to spend the rest of the weekend absorbed in a few good books, maybe even take in a film if there was anything worthwhile showing, and a drink at the pub. Relax, I thought, time to relax. So I took myself out that morning to the local library and browsed for a couple of hours. I finally came away with four books, a wide variety from poetry, novels, to a book on modern Astronomy—an old pastime of mine. I still had the four-inch refractor that I used for stargazing, or more correctly, Moon and planet studying.

SUGAR AND SPICE AND ALL THINGS NICE

The day was warm, but by the time I reached the local it was raining. I sat in the lounge for a while, talking to Tom Gerrard, a neighbour of mine, a pensioner who took time out in the pub most lunch times when the weather wasn't too cold. With a couple of pints of lager inside me and with the atmosphere of the place, I was soon in pleasant conversation with Tom.

'I might be getting old, Doug,' he nodded at me after a lengthy scan of my face, 'but to me you don't half look washed out—like a worn out old rag I'd say.'

Tom was a friendly chap who invariably wore a dark suit, shiny with age, and a waistcoat with a silver pocket watch and chain strung from it. He had a thin, weather-beaten face and his white moustache was yellowed in places from his smoking a pipe.

'I agree,' I said, 'I've been working like the devil the past two weeks, but then, you don't want all the boring details do you?' I smiled.

'Good Lord, no!' he answered in mock consternation, then added, 'I dunno how you do such a thing as indexing. I'll stick to my allotment any day! I 'ad enough of your kind of work when I was setting type for old Barnaby.'

'Not quite the same, though is it Tom—'

'Hmmph. You don't know the half of it,' he said sourly.

And so the day wore on, both of us exchanging pleasantries and gossip until it was chucking-out time. I walked home with Tom and saw him to his gate, where he caught me with a final bit of grapevine news before departing.

'Oh, now did you hear about Mick Geddie's little Sally—gone missing she has. About three weeks now. Only a little mite too. Always used to play hereabouts—always wore a yellow dress.' He paused contemplatively. 'I don't reckon on her chances in this day and age,' he finished with a macabre inflection.

I was glad to say that Tom didn't see my face after he'd said all that. It hit me like a thunderbolt. I knew the Geddies vaguely, but I didn't know their children at all. However, I was sure the girl across the street must have been Sally Geddie. The protruding chin, you see, is a marked characteristic of Mick, her father.

I just couldn't believe it though. I'd seen her only the other day... or was it more than a week ago; I'd lost track of time just recently. But no, it couldn't be the same child. Still, there was a persistent plucking of a chord in my mind that insisted on this girl being the one who was supposed to be missing. I felt like calling in at the police station, but I would be a fool if it turned out to be someone else's daughter I had seen. After all, lots of kids wear yellow dresses. The nightmare I'd had must have mingled with reality until it had heightened the apparent none-event of my original sighting of the girl; without the dream it was a minor incident little worth further thought. I decided not to go to the police.

Instead, I took myself off to the park for the afternoon, with a book to read and sat on a shady bench and dozed and browsed through a few short stories while the sun dried up the rain that had fallen earlier. It might have been an extremely pleasant afternoon, but I was not to be lucky...

I sat almost asleep when I heard a voice call through the bushes behind me: 'Mister... Mister,' it said, 'want to play?' I jerked round startled, and in an instant saw those same penetrating eyes peering at me in their frightening way, but this time I was going to remain calm. Ignoring the stare, I stood up, placing the book on the bench, and said, 'Are you Sally Geddie?' The eyes blinked, the bushes rustled as she moved about and nothing further was said for a short while. Those damnable eyes still remained however, searing my retinas in unholy steadfastness. Then:

'Want to play?' she giggled and leapt out of sight. Further off I heard her shout, 'Hide-and-Seek!'

I decided to put my embarrassment of children aside and join in the game. After all, I had nothing better to do, and if she *was* the missing child—though this now seemed most unlikely—I stood a good chance of reuniting her with her parents. So, I took chase.

A large hollow, ringed with trees and thick bushes and containing a pool of stagnant water lay a few hundred yards distant, and it was towards this that I ran where I saw the telltale yellow dress flying. When I reached the warm air under the trees she was nowhere in sight. I was quite hot and panted heavily while looking here and there in the undergrowth. Then a light, tinkling voice escaped from the greenery, 'You can't find me,' it came in a sing-song manner, tempting, teasing. I moved towards where I thought it came from and there was a rustle of leaves and something yellow slid out of sight. I clawed my way through the thorny bushes but she was gone again.

I was now becoming very warm and a little excited. It was years since I'd done anything like this—yes, it was exciting playing hide-and-seek. All the mystery, the tingling terror of finding and being found, all this welled up from my childhood. I was breathing heavily.

'Sally? Sally?' I said lightly so as not to frighten her, 'Sugar and spice and all things nice! I'm coming to find you!' I passed a huge oak to see the give-away yellow drift past on the other side of the dell. I decided to break out from the trees and run right round the outside of the wooded hollow which would be quicker than negotiating the bushes and ferns, and, as I reached the other side, there came that soft, tormenting voice again, this time a quickly spoken, 'Can't-catch-me!'; then the giggling. I panted. Clearing the trees on the inside I came stumbling down the steep slope to stop by the foul, glistening water at the bottom of the hollow.

Above, the trees made a huge arc, allowing very little direct sunlight in to play on the stagnant water, where insects buzzed incessantly over the surface and strange bubbling sounds broke through from below. Aside from these odd bubblings the water was quite quiescent, black except where a growth of green plants had half covered the surface. It might have been fathoms deep for all one could see into its depths, but in fact it must have been a couple of feet at the most, the bottom probably thick with the mud and the leaf-mould of generations.

The trees down there were weirdly stunted and gnarled old things, infested with fungi, rather different than the tall oaks higher up the slope. The ground was a soft, wet carpet of leaf-mould. It was quiet too, no birds singing down there, though if you listened hard enough, you could hear them chirping high up in the branches, in the light. I sat down on the bank and tossed a twig into the water. It splashed and a few ripples moved sluggishly outwards, then all was silent again. I was acutely aware of my laboured breathing: I had to regain my breath. I was sweating profusely, my brow like a wet and sticky fire causing black spots before my dizzy eyes. I saw no sign of the yellow dress, but something caught my eye in the water. It was the broken-off limb of an oak and it rested, due to its curvature, partly in and partly out of the evil smelling pond. It was absolutely infested with fungus, pale brown pulpy things giving it a hideously soft mantle. Down towards the water the growth was torn and smashed and hung limply into the greasy water, as if someone had pulled, clawed at the rotten fibres in desperation.

I closed my eyes; the dream came back—the door made of fungoid material being ravaged by the girl, her face a mask of hatred... or was it horror? My mind drifted imperceptibly to other things: the heat. It was so damned warm down here amongst the trees, as if the sun's heat of a thousand years had been captured by this murky pool, held in this great dome of oak and chestnut and pine and released in searing gasps when unwary visitors stepped beneath that forbidden place. I wiped the sweat from my forehead. The black spots before my eyes remained. Lack of oxygen, I guessed. Must regain my breath. The heat seemed to be burning my neck now like a fever.

'Can't find me,' breathed a voice, so soft, so quiet now, but even so it startled me.

'Sugar and spice,' I said lazily, too tired to move at the moment, dazzled by visions recurring in my mind. 'Boletus and Toadstool,' I murmured idly.

Something screamed far off.

I looked down, down at the black, turgid waters of the pool, the water lapping at my shoes, leaving vile black detritus on them. My head ached. What was it..? Something was making the usually still waters move. My twig... no, that was minutes ago. Something moving... out there by the tree limb! A brown plastic sandal floated dismally near the edge, green scum licking at its sole.

'She's fallen in!' I screamed, jumping to my feet, my head, my eyes crushed even further by such sudden action. 'Hey, Sally, hey... hey where are you?' The water lapped gently, lapped thickly like obnoxious, noisesome protoplasm. Out there by the fungus-clothed log something yellow swirled in the water curiously. It was too much to bear. She had fallen in and drowned! But I'd been there all the time; there hadn't been a splash. Only... only the faint, *timeless* scream far away.

A face surfaced by the limb, a final confrontation, the water sliding slimily off the pallid features. The face rolled, bloated, soft like the fungi, chin protruding, eyes choked up with green mud. I screamed, scrambling blindly up the steep bank, slipping, falling, making no way at all. It was all my fault. The face still stared, the mouth open, choked with pestiferous, clinging green weed. I found myself back where I began, by the water's edge, tears streaming down my face. My hands were black with the luxuriant earth. I scrambled again and fell back, headlong into the pond. I crawled ashore, sodden, steam rising from my body.

I looked again across the water... there was *nothing.* I sobbed.

'*Can't find me,*' said the voice, '*Can't catch me,*' whispered the voice, spiraling into oblivion!

PROVISIONING

By David Campton

TWO ROCKING CHAIRS creaked slowly on the old porch. Adam's chair creaked more slowly than Keziah's, but Adam was the elder brother—by a good ten minutes. There was a noticeable bald patch in Adam's foxy hair, whereas there were mere streaks of grey in his brother's thatch. 'Pepper n' salt,' giggled Kez when he thought about it. Kez enjoyed a joke, and would often giggle for as long as a week after a good one. Kez was the thrifty one: he liked things to last, even a joke.

The boards of the porch groaned in sympathy as the chairs swayed lazily backwards and forwards.

'Been a thinkin',' said Kez.

Adam's eyes opened, then closed momentarily as he yawned. He settled his great hands behind his head and stared at a cloud as it leisurely crossed the bright sky. The cloud passed.

'Uh-huh?' said Adam.

'Been thinkin' 'bout things we should've been doin',' went on Kez. Kez was the active one. He had ideas, and would sometimes talk about them on and off for days as he rocked on the porch in summer, or by the stove in winter. Kez was the one who thought about getting things done. Adam was more easily satisfied.

'The Lord provides,' said Adam.

'The Lord provides,' echoed Kez, 'But there's still things need to be done. The shingle needs fixin'.'

'Needed fixin' these five years,' agreed Adam.

'I guess a hammer and a few nails would fix it,' said Kez.

'Sure would,' said Adam. He rocked for a few minutes. 'But the Lord will provide. Don't you go aflyin' in the face of the Lord.

There's a good spring o' clear water out back, praise the Lord.'

'Praise the Lord,' responded Kez.

'All we need is that good spring o' clear water out back,' said Adam. He crossed his hands over his belly and closed his eyes, as though exhausted by the conversation.

But Kez was in the mood for talk.

'Worsen a dawg at the moon,' grumbled Adam when his twin persisted.

'There's things,' insisted Kez.

Adam watched a great bird making slow circles in the sky. Had something disturbed it? He pushed the problem to the back of his mind to await a more auspicious moment for rumination.

'Like Betsey,' went on Kez. 'I keep thinkin' 'bout Betsey.'

'I think 'bout Betsey, too, agreed Adam. A great sigh stirred his red, chest-length beard. 'Sometimes I wonder if she thinks 'bout us.'

'We oughta've buried her,' said Kez.

'Yep, we shoulda buried her,' sighed Adam. 'She's been waitin' fer it fer long enough.'

'Her bein' our sister,' continued Kez. 'A sister has a call on a body.'

'S'funny,' murmured Adam. 'As the days go by, I don't seem to notice Betsey so much.'

'Must be nigh on two years.'

'Ain't much left on Betsey now, Hardly worth disturbin' the ground for,'

The rocking continued. Adam watched the trees in the far distance shimmering in the heat haze. The Indian Summer this year seemed to last and last, and there could be no better place than the old porch for soaking up what was left of the sun.

'Pity we had to hit her with the axe.'

Wasn't that just like Kez, gnawing at a topic that had no meat left on it. 'She wouldn't see reason,' said Adam firmly, hoping to kill a conversation that threatened to go on and on.

'Perhaps us hitting Herb Tindy with the axe first had sumpn' to do with it,' mused Kez, "Specially with him lyin' on top of her at the time.'

'She wouldn't see reason,' repeated Adam. 'Screamin' an' screamin'. Botherin' a body. Never could 'bide noise. Herb Tindy never said a word.'

'Guess I took his head near off at the first chop,' went on Kez. 'Guess Betsey was took bad at the blood.'

'She never made no fuss at hog-killin'.'

'But she was never underneath a hog at the time. Guess we ought've waited 'till Herb Tindy climbed offern her.'

'He shoulda waited 'till the proper courting time. Not takin' her on the best bed like he already owned it.'

For a while the brothers rocked in unison, remembering.

'Anyway,' said Adam at last, 'she's had that best bed ever since.'

Overhead in the silent air circled the great bird, watching for carrion.

'Perhaps we shoulda buried her at the time,' said Kez.

The way the man went on about burying. 'Perhaps we shoulda eaten her,' said Adam sharply. 'The way we did Herb Tindy.'

'The dawg sure appreciated them bones,' chuckled Kez appreciatively.

'The Lord will provide,' pronounced Adam.

'The Lord will provide,' came the response. 'I guess Herb Tindy was what you'd call a sign 'cause, the Lord has gone on providin' for us ever since.'

The peace of the afternoon was broken. Adam could see that Kez was set on talking, and there would be no dozing for anybody until he had talked himself to a stop.

'Jus' like he said,' confirmed Adam, stretching his bear-like arms. 'Jus' you sit back, you brothers,' says the Lord. 'You done a good job in takin' that couple in 'dultery, an' to show my 'preciation I'm agoin' to have fresh meat delivered to your door whenever you're in need. And the Lord has been as good as his word, Praise the Lord.'

'Praise the Lord,' cried Kez 'The dawg sure appreciates them bones.'

The afternoon was still again. No breeze rustled the dried grass around the porch. An acute ear might have caught the sound of a dog scratching himself, or of the spring bubbling behind the shack. A sharp eye might have spied movement on the road a couple of miles below. But Adam sank his fifteen stone into his chair and plied the rockers.

Kez whistled soundlessly. He was still thinking. 'Hope the Lord ain't gettin' absent-minded,' he said at last. 'Near a month since we had fresh meat.'

'There's always the good spring o' cool, clear water. Cool clear spring water makes good drinkin'.'

'But kinda thin eatin',' mumbled Kez.

'Don't you go questioning the ways of the Lord.' Adam was unusually sharp. 'You don't want Him withdrawin' his appreciation now. The Lord provides. Remember the time when we was near starvin' with nothin' but a cup o' berries between us. What did the Lord do? The Lord sent a Boy Scout aknockin' at the door.'

'Tender young shoat,' murmured Kez.

'And with a whole stock of canned beans in his pack.'

'Mighty tasty beans,' reminisced Kez.

'And didn't the lord send the whole campin' o' scouts around afterwards, askin' after him?'

'One by one,' agreed Kez. 'Kep' us eatin' the whole winter. Lucky we kep' that barrel o' salt in the back.'

Adam suddenly raised his hand, commanding silence. On the

road below the sun glinted on the windscreen of a car. The sound of its engine could just be beard labouring up the hill.

'The lord sure is quick to answer,' grinned Kez.

'Fresh meat,' said Adam. His eyes were suddenly sharp and alert. All traces of his recent sleepiness vanished.

'Wonder if he'll have any beans with him?' mused Kez,

'Don't you go aquestioning the Lord's provisioning arrangements,' snapped Adam.

'I ain't aquestioning nothin',' protested Kez, 'I was just athinkin' how beans can be tasty.'

'The Lord provides,' intoned Adam.

'The Lord provides,' responded Kez.

The car could be heard rasping and choking along the dusty road. In it the driver cursed the map that had rated this second-class mule trail as a usable road. For over two thousand miles he had run over mountain and through desert, avowedly trying to forget, but in fact damning divorce, damning alimony, damning community property laws, damning over-eager juniors anxious to edge a man from his hard-won place atop the ladder, damning doctors who could not reverse time at fifty, damning anything and everything in his path; hoping that the minor irritations of thirst, mosquitoes, and rough living might distract from the greater pain at the back of his mind; but having even that last hope dashed.

However he still had enough breath to swear at the white dust that stung his eyes, caked on his lips, and clogged his nose. His rich and varied oaths stirred a faint ghost of the sergeant (decorated in Korea) buried under the layers of fat accumulated while sitting around in executive suites. That sergeant would not be floored forever by the double defeat in bed and board-room. That sergeant would come back swinging. Even as he swore, he noticed the shack.

It was a crazily derelict heap of boards, held together more by habit than joinery. It could hardly have been a human habitation. Yet a solitary man stood hoeing a patch in front of the porch.

The car stopped. The man was intent on his work, and presumably had not heard. At any rate he paid no heed, but continued leisurely to ply his hoe. The shack was set back over a hundred yards from the road, and little more could be made of the worker except that he wore ragged denims, and his carroty hair glowed in the sunlight.

The driver rubbed the excess dust from his spectacles, and looked again. Still the man with the hoe disregarded him.

'Hi, there! Hi!'

The movement of the hoe slowed to a stop. There was a pause for a count of about forty, as though the red-head were deciding whether he had really heard anything: then he turned. Shading his eyes against the sun, he peered at the car. At last he ambled towards it. The driver waved as the ragged denims approached.

'Howdy, Tindy,' shouted the red-head.

'Tindy?' Something besides the greeting puzzled the driver. In spite of the heat there was no sweat on the red-head's face; in spite of his work no dust on the stubble. Perhaps out here they were so used to discomfort that it had no effect on them. The ex-sergeant was again reminded of what years of soft living had done to him.

'Glad t'see y'again, Tindy,' grinned the red-head.

'I'm not Tindy,' said the driver.

'Not Tindy?'

'My name isn't Tindy,' rasped the driver; then regretting his irritation, 'it's—er—it's Driver.'

'Driver, huh?'

'Driver.'

'I'm Keziah. Call me Kez.'

'Can I get to Stotetown this way?'

'I coulda took an oath as you was Herby Tindy.'

'I'm trying to...'

'O' course, now I come to look at you, I can see you're not.'

'Tell me...'

'You're younger than Tindy. Better kept. Herb Tindy was kinda scrawny.'

Driver closed his eyes and grasped the steering wheel, clicking back the rising anger, not listening to the musing drawl.

'You're nicer rounded. Like to see a rounded man. A man oughta have plenty of flesh on his bones. Weren't moren' a mouthful on old Tindy.'

Even when Driver heard the words they seemed to have no meaning. The sound added up to no more than the buzzing of a lazy fly. 'Flesh,' the hayseed had seemed to say. 'Mouthful.'

Driver turned to Kez, and was faced with a gleaming smileful of white teeth. The fool was friendly, and was entitled at least to a civil answer.

'What did you say?' asked Driver.

'You aiming to sell sumpn'?' said Kez. 'We ain't got much to offer in return 'cept a few old roots.'

'I'm not selling anything,' replied Driver.

'Beans, now,' went on Kez. 'I guess you ain't got no canned beans in back there.'

'No beans,' confirmed Driver.

'Beans make mighty tasty eatin',' said Kez. 'But if you ain't sellin' anything, I guess you'll be wanting sumpn'.'

'I want...'

'Aw!' A bellow of laughter interrupted Driver, and Kez clapped his hands with sudden understanding. 'Now I know what you want. You'll be wantin' a drink o' cool, clear, water.'

'No.'

'Our cool, clear, spring water makes mighty good drinkin'.'

'All I want is direction. Does this godawful apology for a road take me to Stotetown?'

'Sure. Sure. The only place it will take you to. Thought youda known that, drivin' this way.'

'Thank you.'

'Ten miles or more on, and it's a mighty dusty track. Sure you wouldn't care for that drink o' water. Comes bubblin' up freshn' cold. O'course I ain't pushin' it on you, neighbour; but I guess it's kinda neighbourly to offer— specially to a body as parched-up as you look. It's free to us—it's free to you, neighbour. The Lord provides.'

The thought of water sparked Driver's imagination. Cold water frosting a glass. Water trickling down a parched throat. Water that might even sluice away regrets, bad dreams, and soured ambitions even as it washed away the sweat and dust. For a second he thought he glimpsed something for which he had been searching. It couldn't really be as simple as a drink on a scorching day, and yet...

'Thanks,' he said, and slid from the car.

Kez jerked his head. 'Back o' the shack. Foller me,'

But even as Driver stumbled after the lumbering red-head over the broken ground, the euphoria faded. The cynic at the back of his mind with whose help he had outsmarted his associates and beaten back his competitors, began to whisper. Nobody ever does anything for nothing. Nothing is for free. In the long run a gift costs more than the goods you pay for. What did the friendly scarecrow hope to get in return for his drink of water? If Driver ever offered a drink of water there would be strings attached. Why should there be one law for the city, and another for the backwoods?

Driver tripped against the hoe left lying on the baked ground, and stifled the mild blasphemy that he automatically voiced.

Kez turned to see Driver frowning at the rusty head and rough, near-black handle, Kes was disappointed that Driver had halted. So far everything had worked so smoothly. No fish had ever risen so daintily to the bait. Only a few yards more to the invitingly open door, and everything would be over bar the gutting and jointing.

'C'mon, mister,' urged Kez. 'Y'want that water?'

'Dropped your hoe,' observed Driver, prodding it with his shoe toe.

'Pick it up on the way back,' replied Kez. 'C'mon.'

But Driver did not move. Intuition is a matter of subconsciously interpreting signs and portents. In Korea the sergeant had picked off the sniper before the sniper had dropped him. In business he had forecast market trends before they hit the Dow Jones Index. There was something wrong about that hoe.

'Thought you was in a hurry to get to Stotetown,' grumbled Kez,

'You in a hurry?' asked Driver.

'Got all day,' replied Kez. 'Thought you was thirsty. Don't act like you was thirsty.' The sun glinted on Driver's glasses, obscuring his piggy eyes. It bothered Kez that he couldn't see those eyes.

The hoe worried Driver. It had a significance that eluded him. Like—well, like a wife grown smugly contented after months of wild-cat spitting and scratching; and he hadn't suspected that another man was servicing her. Like those mislaid files of accounts that suddenly turned up in the enemy's office. It seemed as though the fat that encased his body was also smothering his mind. Think. Think! Why should a man be hoeing when any reasonable creature would be taking refuge from the sun? Why hoe a barren patch at this time of year? It wasn't as if the red-head liked work, otherwise the shack wouldn't be falling apart. Feeling the pricking down his spine, the sergeant would have reached for his gun: but there was no longer a gun handy—this was a different time, a different world, perhaps a different man. He glanced to where his car was parked, eighty or so yards away.

'You ain't agoin' back?' said Kez anxiously. 'Not without that water.' Then, conscious that he may have sounded over-eager, 'Best water in these parts.'

Driver was conscious of the bill-fold tightly wedged into his hip pocket. He realized that he would be lucky if he managed to get away without losing that wad of notes. It was not the possible loss of money, but of face, that worried him. He'd sound such a fool, trying to explain to a flint-eyed cop that he'd fallen victim to this red-faced clod. He couldn't do it.

'No. I'm following you,' smiled Driver with tight lips. In a race for the car his podgy body would be no match against the rangey limbs of his companion. The game had to be played through. 'Lead on,' he said.

Kez led the way to the open door.

'You set yourself down in there,' he said. 'I'll fetch the water from round back. The cup's kinda cracked, but I guess you won't mind that.'

'I'll come with you,' said Driver.

'Thought you might like to set out o' the sun,' said Kez.

'Glad of the chance to stretch my legs,' replied Driver.

Kez glanced appealingly at the open door. This was not the way it should happen. Usually the meat walked meekly through the door, behind which Adam stood with axe upraised.

Already Adam's arms were beginning to tire. He had held the axe aloft from the minute he heard footsteps on the path. Kez went barefoot until the first snows, so the steps could only belong to a well-shod stranger. They were heavy footsteps, too—a well-fed stranger. But the footsteps had halted, and talk was going on. What cause had Kez to stop for talk when he knew Adam was waiting with axe upraised? It was a heavy axe, and Adam's arms began to shake a little; yet he durst not lower the weapon for fear of the stranger walking in before he had time to raise it again. That might lead to a struggle, and Adam did not like struggling—last year one of the scouts had delivered a vicious kick, and Adam had limped for days. He thought obscenities at Kez, who talked and talked while the axe grew heavier.

'You could set on the porch awhile,' be heard Kez say. 'Mighty comfortable chair for rockin'.'

'I've been sitting for long enough,' replied the stranger, cheerfully obstinate. 'You live here alone?'

'Jus' me an' the dawg,' replied Kez, preferring that the stranger should not suspect that someone might be waiting with an axe.

'Two chairs,' pointed out the stranger.

'Oh, them,' said Kez. Then his voice brightened. 'Sometimes I set in the one. Sometimes I set in the other. Mighty comfortable chairs. C'mon through the house.'

'The spring's round the back,' remarked the stranger.

'Sure,' said Kez. 'Cool, clear, spring water. The Lord provides.'

'Then I'll walk round outside,' said the stranger. 'Shoes are dusty. Wouldn't want to trample dirt inside your house.'

Adam's muscles were screaming for respite. Soon he would either have to lower the axe or drop it. Sweat trickled into the corner of his eye.

'Walk round outside,' echoed Kez unhappily. He raised his voice, hoping that Adam would hear and deal with the change of plan. 'To th'back. I guess the dawg'll be waiting for us round the corner, but you've no cause to fear the dawg.'

At last Adam lowered the axe. With unusual agility, considering his fifteen stone, he hurried through the shack, past the bedroom where Betsey lay, and through the back door. As he took up his position by the wall, and raised the axe again, approaching voices could already be heard.

'Appreciate what you're doing for me, neighbour,' the stranger was saying.

'The Lord provides,' responded Kez automatically.

Adam edged forward. One good downward blow would be sufficient, and out here there would be less mess to clear up. Then the stranger seemed to stand still again.

Driver's long-dormant combat instinct was stirring. Ahead lay a blind corner. Instinctively Driver wanted to take it in a wide sweep to avoid any possible ambush; but the red-head was crowding him, almost pushing him against the wall. Between the red-head and the wall there was no room to maneuver, no freedom to use his arms. To give himself time to plan, Driver stopped by a window.

'Looks like the frame needs work,' he remarked casually.

'One o' these days,' murmured Kez. 'Was just a'sayin' there's things need to be done.'

'Saying?'

'To th'dawg.'

'Intelligent dog.'

Driver tried to glance through the window, but the glass was so grimed that nothing but a blur could be seen beyond; a whitish blob that could have been a bed in the middle of the room.

Kez noticed the glance. Nothing was happening as it should. It was almost as bad as the time when they had to chase the scout and cut his throat in the woods. He had screamed and struggled. If they weren't careful, this one might scream and struggle too. This one had to be reassured about the things he had seen through the window. But when he spoke, Keziah's voice was strained.

'Guess that's Betsey,' he croaked. 'You don't have to worry none 'bout Betsey.'

'Betsey?'

The last pane of glass was broken. Kez had meant to fix it some time, but they never used the room, and Betsey wouldn't mind.

Driver peered through the hole.

In contrast to the bright sunlight outside, the room was in shadow; but this made the bed in the middle of the room so much more conspicuous. The coverings had once been white, except where great, dark stains were splashed. A thick film of grey dust covered everything, so at first it was not easy to make out what lay on the bed. It had a human form—if human can be taken to mean a mere structure of bones covered like a drum with parchment skin. Judging by the flowing hair the thing on the bed had once been a girl: but should any girl be holding her head in her hands? — especially when that head rested on her navel.

Slack-jawed, Driver turned from the window to find himself staring into the florid, shining face of Kez.

'Said there's things needin' to be fixed,' muttered Kez apologetically.

Driver's scream was like a trapped animal. Kez was taken aback by it, knowing that he hadn't even touched the man. Driver turned and ran. He had reached the porch before Kez had gathered his wits sufficiently to act.

Hearing the cry Adam leaped out from behind the shack. He did not wait for explanations, but seeing the stranger hurtling away, pounded after him. Kez followed.

Driver could not piece together the situation. At this time he did not want to. His one concern was to get away from the shack and everyone and everything in it as soon as he could. He kicked the hoe left lying in front of the porch, and lost valuable seconds as he paused to grab it up. It was a poor weapon, but better than bare hands. Then he heard shouts behind him as he fled towards the car.

His breath whistled painfully in his throat, his chest seemed clamped in a vice unable to admit more air; an ache spread from his calves to his ankles; his feet might have been encased in leaden boots, rising and falling as slowly as in a nightmare; and he knew that, even with the few yards advantage he had snatched, he could not reach the car. He turned at bay.

A wild giant with a chest-length beard that flared red bore down on him. This monster, with massive shoulders and a waist like an oak, brandished an axe that might have felled a sapling at a blow. The creature screeched furiously, and with the lunacy that survives in the numb corner of a terrified mind, Driver thought of a baby whose bottle has been taken away.

For a second Driver stared at death as he had done year's before. Then, with a click, another man seemed to take over; a man used to finding a bayonet in his hands. Automatically he thrust the hoe at the exposed navel of the giant, who being no more than a man, bent double, winded. Adam fell forward, and the axe flew from his hands, skimming over the hard ground to come to rest a couple of yards away from the car.

Driver pounced upon it. When he straightened up, Kez was hardly more than an arm's length away, staring incredulously. The axe whirled, and a head bounced along the ground. The body swayed; then as twin founts of blood spouted from the neck, Kez fell across his brother, who writhed and moaned in the dirt.

Driver dropped the axe, turned, and stumbled idiot-faced towards his car. Dull-eyed and openmouthed, relying on habit to pilot him, he fell into the driving seat and turned the ignition key. No-one stopped him as he drove away. The sound of the engine faded, and the white dust settled again.

For a while Adam lay still. The discomfort had passed, and he would have liked to sleep; but the ground was hard and gritty, there was a weight on his back, and some hot, sticky liquid had been poured over him. He stirred, then sat up.

His brother's body rolled over. His brother's head, still incredulous, stared at him. Adam stared back.

'I guess that was your fault, Kez,' he said at last. 'Goin' on 'bout them canned beans. If the Lord had meant beans fer eatin' they'd walk on legs just like you'r me.'

He stood up and rubbed his bruised belly.

'That's what comes of questioning the Lord's provisioning arrangements,' he went on. 'Looks like we'll be eatin' this winter, Kez, but you won't be sharin .'

He put his hands under his brother's shoulders, and began to drag the body towards the shack. 'The Lord provides,' he cried.

One of these days he would go back and pick up the head.

'Praise the Lord!'

THE SATYR'S HEAD: TALES OF TERROR

PERFECT LADY

By Robin Smyth

I DON'T KNOW WHETHER to jump. It's a long way down.
Long way from the roof to the ground. Twenty-one storeys. And
at the bottom it's all those concrete pillars. What a mess I'll be in.
Makes you go cold just to think about it. Still, without my Winnie,
life's going to be all hairshirts and sourberries and I'll never get my
Winnie back now. I saw them wheeling her out of the garden in
her chair. Two big policemen. They looked ever so small from up
here. Like shadows on the stone. They don't realize what they've
done to me those policemen, taking my Winnie away like this. I
mean, what has my Winnie ever done to deserve such treatment?
She's a very nice girl. Perfect lady. Never nags. Just accepts her role
in life as a servant to the male. It's going to be terrible without her.
No more cuddles on winter's nights. No more kissing on the sofa.
No more reclining on the rug listening to Beethoven together. I like
Beethoven, I do. Winnie does too. Everything I like, Winnie likes.
And that's as it should be.

God, it is a long way down and there's a cold wind blowing
across the river from Fulham way. Suppose I did jump and the
wind caught me and tossed me into the branches of that oak down
there. I'd be impaled. That'd hurt. Perhaps it wouldn't be right to
jump. Not a man of my age. Thirty-six. So young. Be a crime
against humanity. Poor, dear Winnie. I wonder what they'll do to
her. I bet that Lizzie Spring's got something to do with it. I
wouldn't be surprised. She's a funny woman that Lizzie Spring.

I loved her, Lizzie Spring. Long before I got Winnie of course.
Long before. But I did love her. Yes, I did. From the moment I
spotted her in the automatic laundry place down Lillie Road one

January evening. I thought she was I the loveliest, most desirable creature I'd clapped eyes on since Marilyn Monroe in *The Seven Year Itch*.

She was blonde and doll-like and as feminine as a lace handker-chief and I wondered if I dared talk to her. I was going on thirty two at the time and though I wore rather thick-lensed glasses and had a slight limp due to childhood rickets and a lump on my neck which was not noticeable when I bad my coat collar turned up, I was quite handsome in a journalistic sort of way. Kind of a Scoop McCoy, Fleet Street special reporter type, if you get my meaning. I always parted my hair down the middle and I would brush it with Brylcreem till it shone and though my blue stripe suit was a wee bit threadbare about the elbows, it was nonetheless clean, as were my brown brogues and my shirt collar. One thing my mother always taught me... no matter how shabby your attire, if it was clean the world would respect you. Mind you, I never got much respect from the world. Not in general. If they'd thought I was rich... well... they wouldn't have laughed at me like they did... but they didn't think I was rich so they just kept on and on. Whisper-ing.

In the office of Baldry and Blacker, the Cornhill seed merchants where I worked before Mummy and Daddy passed on, the clerks used to call me Squinty instead of Rupert, which is my true name. And the typists used to laugh at me a lot. Because of my limp, and also because of a big, brown birthmark which stuck to one side of my face like some giant, furry beetle. They never knew that I could see them laughing. But I did. Oh yes. Lizzie never laughed at me. She told me that she could see in me the soul of a poet and I explained that this was probably because my heart was bent on a literary career rather than that of a pen pusher in a seed factory. I courted her for several months and when the first warm days of spring skipped in to cheer the year, I proposed that we be married.

Lizzie was delighted and for the first time since we met she kissed me. Not a long, soft, passionate kiss but a sweet, ladylike touch upon my birthmark, an action which caused my blood to run cold and my heart to beat wildly in my chest.

I've never understood why she went and eloped with this bloke Georgie Milford out of Dingwell's garage in the Fulham Palace Road. I do realize that a lot of it was due to my Mummy and Daddy. They only met her once, but they hated her on sight and said she was nothing but a slut... a gold-digging slut... but Lizzie did love me, she told me so often... so why she went off the way she did completely bamboozles my imagination.

It was so sudden. One minute she was my betrothed... and the next she was hot-footing off with this excuse for a garage mechanic. He was six feet odd, blond and bearded and apparently he used to try a spot of this weight-lifting caper in his spare time. The man was an ox. An illiterate, ill-bred ox. Lizzie met him at Further Education classes apparently and Lord only knows what lies he told her to entice her away from me but they wound up flitting off to some new town in Herefordshire where they were given a council house, garden back and front at the expense of rate-payers like muggins. I can tell you truly I was very upset. Very upset indeed because I always thought that Lizzie was the perfect lady. But she was nothing less than a two-timing, underhanded little hussy and I can tell you I was in half a mind to go down to that there Herefordshire and do something. Pay her back. Throw a drop of acid at her or something. You know, throw it in her face. Scar her a bit. Make her pay. The vicious, ungrateful little hussy.

Still, I was well rid of that little tramp. I decided in my heart that I would not ally myself with any such painted hussies again but I would search for... well, a plainer, more reliable type. Someone you could trust. Put your faith in. A kind of perfect lady if you like.

I met Daphne in the Hammersmith Bingo Hall. She was a Midlands girl from. Hanley, Stoke-on-Trent. About forty. She had blue eyes and a thin face and little hairs curling from her chin and she possessed a distinct body smell which was in its own way quite attractive. Yet there was about her one thing which reminded me of that slattern, Lizzie. Her hair. It was soft and natural blonde and hung about her shoulders like silken bubbles. Very nice. We got talking and after Bingo we walked slowly together through the back doubles towards her digs in Greyhound Road. She didn't stop talking for one second. Talk, talk, talk, in this horrible nasal accent of hers. If it hadn't been for that gorgeous head of hair, I'm sure I would have fled from her after the first five eternal minutes. But it fascinated me. That hair. It didn't really belong to her. Didn't suit her. She wasn't fitted to keep it. Hair so beautiful was created for Lizzie, though I'm not praising Lizzie in any way of course, she was what she was and that's that... but the more I stared at this shining glory of pale gold on this ugly head, the more I realized that I had a duty to perform... that head of hair just had to be rescued from that talkative head.

With my four-bladed penknife, which I've carried since I was a lad in Beaver patrol of the 29th Fulham, I slit Daphne's throat. So swiftly and expertly that she hardly gurgled as she slithered from my loving embrace. Then with infinite care, I knelt beside her and gradually sawed the scalp from her noggin. She looked really horrible laying there all dead and bald, so I dragged her to a wheelbarrow which some builder had left in this dark and narrow alley and I dumped her body in that barrow and covered her gently with some dusty cement sacks to protect her from the rain and marauding rats, then tucking the warm and bloody head of hair under my raincoat, I hastened home.

I met loads of girls after that. There was Mildred from Hemel Hempstead, who had the most beautiful brown eyes I've ever seen, well, I should say the second most beautiful pair really, because Lizzie Spring's were the most beautiful; that I must confess, even though we all know what a tramp that Lizzie was. I used to like looking into Mildred's eyes, admiring them... but I couldn't stand her stutter. Couldn't say two words on the run without hissing and stumbling like an idiot woman and after two whole nights of miserable courting I took her for a stroll along the Putney towing path where I cleverly garroted her with a rusty cheese wire which had fallen into my possession. I lay her carefully on the damp night grass and very tenderly I gouged out those fascinating eyes with a teaspoon which I had brought along for that very purpose, then I tipped her in the swollen river and, with brown eyes carefully wrapped in tissue paper and popped into an Old Holborn Inn, I made my way home where I transferred the eyes to a jar of pickling vinegar and put them on a shelf in the pantry right close to Daphne's head of hair which I kept, brushed and washed daily, under a Stilton cheese dish which had once belonged to my grandmother.

Now although I might have earlier hinted at it, I never exactly told you that I am quite the little rich man. All inherited of course from Mummy and Daddy. Mummy and Daddy died quite suddenly you see, a couple of years back (not long after Lizzie done the dirty on me in fact)... died after their car brakes failed when travelling down a mountain roadside in Wales where we had gone for a month's holiday. Luckily, I had stayed behind in the hotel at Aberystwyth looking at my stamp collection of British and Commonwealth commemoratives, else I too would have joined them in that ghastly five thousand feet plunge to eternity. Mummy and Daddy left me this house on Lavender Hill, which is big and Victorian, two others in the better part of Chelsea, a portfolio of the most excellent shares and sixteen thousand, eight hundred pounds in cash. Yes, they left me very comfortable.

I often wonder, you know, if it was my wealth, or rather my one
-day-to-be-inherited wealth, which so attracted that strumpet
Lizzio to me and not my looks and personality as she would have
me believe, because I can strongly recall that my opening gambit to
this Jezebel of the washing machine shop was. 'Hi, babe, how'd
you fancy getting hooked up with a millionaire?' And her eyes,
those lovely brown eyes, just sparkled with LSD signs. She
pursued the subject and when I told her all about Mummy and
Daddy and their piles of loot, she all but volunteered to accompany
me to the Victoria and Albert museum the following evening for a
night out. Still, why should I care what her stinking attitudes
were. I don't even want to think about that harlot... feature for
feature she doesn't even compare with my Winnie.

Penelope was a young lass from Carlisle way whom I met at
West Brompton underground station. She was just getting on and
I was just getting off, but some strange compulsion made me do a
swift about turn and leap back into the train to land like some
white knight errant beside her. We got to chatting about the
weather and money and work, and by the time we arrived at
Liverpool Street station, I'd given her a tenner as she told me some
very sad story about not being able to afford a maxi coat for the
winter, and we were indeed on the most intimate terms, I
arranging to meet her from her place of work that very afternoon.

Penelope had the milkiest, whitest arms in this whole wide
world. Really soft and lovely they were. Cream satin. It seemed
impossible to believe that such a broomstick of a girl, with such a
coarse complexion and truly horrible manners could possess these
lovely arms. God, it would appear, had made a criminal error and I
felt bound to put the matter right.

She died very quickly from a stab wound in the back, the knife
thrust up and twisted to severely pierce the heart. She was at the
time sitting in the dining room of my place in Lavender Hill,

enjoying a meal of sweet and sour pork and chow mein which I had bought at Foo Ling's takeaway Chinese shop just down the road.

Those beautiful arms were very hard to remove. Without damaging them, that is... but I managed quite nicely with a sharpened carving knife and a fine-bladed hacksaw and soon Penelope's arms were floating in preserving fluid in my old aquarium, next to the hair of Daphne and the eyes of Mildred. Penelope's ugly remains went into the cupboard under my back stairs.

Well, as the months went by, I searched diligently for my perfect lady, but to no avail. Alice from Camden Town had perfect breasts... and nothing else. Cicely from Swanage had the daintiest feet. Moira from Australia had the sweetest ears and I've never seen legs quite so perfect as Joyce's from Enfield... except maybe Lizzie Spring's. There I was with all the bits and pieces but no entire, floating forlornly in my well-stocked larder.

Then it happened.

One evening when I was inspecting my handsome collection of perfect parts, a hobby which as you may gather had superseded my old one of stamp collecting, an inspiring idea exploded in my mind. Why I hadn't thought of it before, I'll never know, yet I came to realize that the inkling of it had always been tucked away somewhere in my dark subconscious... and this was the reason I had collected all these lovely bits together.

Being as the perfect lady is almost impossible to find, why not, Rupert, I thought, create your own.

Why not be your own God and create your own woman? Eh?

And that was how Winnie came to be created. From a superstructure of wire, plastic, glue and wood, endowed with Mildred's eyes and special rubber lips, Penelope's tender arms, hinged and stitched with leather tabs so that they could cuddle me, Moira's ears to whisper into, Alice's soft breasts, Joyce's long legs, Cicely's neat little feet and Daphne's soft, golden hair my perfect lady was born.

I called her Winnie after my dear mother. Winnie's such a homely name. I bought her all the latest clothes from Marks and Sparks and I sent up for lots of daring underwear from mail order houses. Winnie was pleased.

I played Monopoly with her. And Scrabble. And Beat Your Neighbours Out Of Doors. And I tried to teach her Chess... but the dear, sweet girl just couldn't get the hang of it. I loved my Winnie. Truly loved her. I would kiss her and cuddle her and take her to bed on cold nights and snuggle up to her. I even bought an electric blanket because her arms were so cold at times. Yes, I loved her... and I know she loved me back. I could tell by the look in her big, brown eyes when I used to stroke her hair and fondle her ears.

Winnie enjoyed the good things of life, as indeed I do, but that which she liked best of all was when I used to take her out in grandma's old wheelchair which had lain in the cellar for thirty years or more.

I used to take her shopping in Clapham junction and lots of people used to stare quite rudely so I bought Winnie a pretty hat with a black veil and I used to wrap her up warmly in a big check blanket and we would go for strolls around Arding and Hobbs looking in the babywear department, the sad thing being that Winnie could never have children and I know it must have hurt her deeply looking at all those nappies and shawls and bouncing baby swings. I should never have taken her really.

Yes Winnie and me were happy, but people are so vindictive. So evil and jealous. People just can't leave well alone. Some people just don't like to see other people happy. Just don't. And it's people that's brought us to this present unhappy predicament.

I had a slight accident, you see, just outside my front garden gate. I was pushing Winnie home after an outing to the ponds on the Common where we'd had a lovely afternoon feeding the duckies and enjoying the sunshine, when suddenly, just as I was turning into the garden, the offside wheel of Winnie's wheelchair caught a large stone. I couldn't control the chair and it tipped sideways and poor Winnie was hurled to the pavement.

As fate would have it, two old crows, one of whom I recognized as Mrs. Flately, a shrew from further down the road, the other being Mrs. O'Dell, her nosey next door neighbour, came passing by. Well the screams they uttered must have pierced the very roof of Heaven and sent the Devil in Hell scurrying for cover. They dropped their bags of shopping and raced away, arms flailing, feet thudding as I, muttering how sorry I was, picked up the odds and ends which had dropped from my dear Winnie, including an eye which had rolled to the gutter and a leg which was being sniffed at by a mangy dog.

Hastily I bundled Winnie into the chair, not waiting to fix her together properly, and I hurried inside, bolting the door.

There were police in my front garden and people outside my front gate. Ugly people. A mob. Screaming obscenities. Throwing stones and bottles and the so-called guardians of the law hardly deigning to stop them. My God, I don't know what this country's coming to. There's just no freedom or privacy of the individual anymore.

I watched from the attic window, peering down at that screaming mass of boorish louts and uncouth women. They were shouting. Yelling. Filthily swearing.

'Get the murdering bastard!' yelled one.

'String 'im up!'

'Burn the ghoul!'

Then one of them spotted me. 'There he is. Get 'im!' And the police collapsed under the mastodon-like power of the crowd. And they all surged forward smashing at my house with bricks and sticks and lumps of iron. I escaped over the rooftops, hopping like some poor squirrel pursued by wolves. Through a window and down a drainpipe and then I was running towards the tower blocks of the new council estate.

They've put Winnie in a black van now and locked the doors. She'll be frightened in there. It must be dark. I wonder why Lizzie went and left me like she did. Lizzie! LIIII... ZZZZZIIE!

It's like being a sparrow up here. A warm, plump little sparrow perched on a ledge. Or an eagle.

They're marching down the street now. Thousands of evil people. They mean me harm. Those Lilliputians.

I don't know whether to jump.

I don't know.

THE BUSINESS ABOUT FRED

By Joseph Payne Brennan

AT THE TIME I was a cub reporter on the local *Star Daily*, a morning paper. Unless something "big" was still breaking, I'd usually leave the editorial rooms shortly before midnight. I drifted into a regular routine; six nights out of seven I'd stop in at Casserman's Cafe and drink beer until the place closed at one. A few other newspapermen would stop in; we'd talk and unbend for an hour before going home to bed.

Casserman's was a quiet place. I suppose it was like a thousand other bars. I can't remember a single outstanding or remarkable thing about it unless it might be the autographed, framed photograph of Jack Dempsey prominently displayed over the cash register. But on second thought I guess at least several hundred other bars had framed autographed photographs of Jack Dempsey.

Casserman was friendly but not ebullient. If you felt like talking, he'd lend a listening ear. If you didn't want to talk, he'd respect your silence. He kept the place reasonably clean and he wouldn't tolerate real rowdiness. It was just a pleasantly drab little refuge to relax in about midnight.

Around this time of night, one of the fixtures of the place was a runty-looking guy whom Casserman addressed as Fred. He resembled a disbarred jockey or a down-at-heels tout, pale-faced, shifty-eyed and always taciturn. He'd just sit hunched up over a beer and never say a word, but his eyes couldn't stay put.

After awhile we paid no more attention to him than we did to the photograph of Jack Dempsey. His eyes would flick around the place and sometimes sort of accidentally meet your own, but there was never any challenge in them. They seemed vacant, incurious, oddly cold, and they slid away without revealing anything. The pale, wedge-shaped face never showed any expression.

Casserman told us once that he thought his silent customer had something to do with horse racing and "different sports events", but be was vague about it and none of us were interested enough to make any further inquiries.

The months and finally several years passed. I got a city-room promotion and a raise in pay. Several of my reporter friends left and several others took their places. And almost every night, about twelve, I went to Casserman's and drank beer. And every night when I went there, Fred, the runty little guy with the pale wedge of a face, sat at the end of the bar and silently sipped his beer. His eyes roved around as always, restless but empty looking. Sometimes I'd give him a short nod when I first went in but I never could figure out whether or not he gave a half nod in reply. If he did, it was scarcely perceptible. I never saw him talking to anyone except Casserman and even then only a few perfunctory words were exchanged.

As time went on, the funny little runt seemed to get whiter and smaller and more silent—if that was possible. He seemed to be shrinking. I'd never paid any attention to his clothes, but I finally noticed one evening how really seedy they had become. All this registered in a sort of subconscious way. I had no real interest in the character. Several times during the evening you'd catch his eyes sliding away, but they affected me no more than the blinking neon sign across the street.

More time passed. Six months. Eight months. I can't remember precisely. I went to Casserman's as usual and drank beer and as always the runt sat at the far end of the bar, pale and still and shrunken-looking. He just seemed to be fading away.

One evening, toward the end, I caught his eyes sliding away and, just momentarily, something about his expression held my attention. Had I read a kind of fleeting but desperate appeal in those shifty eyes, or had I only imagined it? I was troubled, briefly, and then one of my cronies came in and we started to talk and I forgot all about the runt.

From here on, it's tough. The time sequence and the exact sequence of minor events.

One evening, I remember, Casserman leaned across the bar and shook his head. 'Fred's lookin' bad. Real bad. And not touchin' his beer.'

I glanced toward the end of the bar. Fred sat there as usual and, to be truthful, he looked about the same to me. No worse than usual, that is. What I do remember is that the light at the far end of the bar appeared to be a bit dimmer than it ordinarily was. I couldn't seem to get a sharp clear image of Fred. But the room was pretty smoky at the time and I thought nothing of it. I made some reply to Casserman, glanced up to see if a bulb had burned out— apparently none had—and then turned toward the door as my friend, Henry Kalk, the rewrite man, came in.

Two or three nights later Casserman leaned over and shook his head again. 'I guess Fred's gettin' worse.'

I looked toward the end of the bar. Fred was no longer there. I was startled; the little runt almost never left till closing time.

'I didn't see him leave,' I said rather pointlessly.

Casserman's big shoulders bunched. 'Left without touchin' his beer.' A wry grin turned the corners of his mouth. 'And didn't leave any dime either!'

For a few minutes, before the rest of the gang came in, I thought about Fred. He was obviously sick and something should be done. I resolved to ask about him somewhere. Then the city room slaves burst in and I'm afraid I forgot all about it as usual.

But the next night, when I returned to my midnight refuge, I did recall Casserman's comment. I looked toward the end of the bar and there sat Fred as usual, still and white. He glanced up and then quickly looked away and I was rather shocked at his appearance. His face seemed terribly drawn and sunken; he appeared years older than he had a few weeks before. I got the impression that he was seriously ill and just going ahead on will power alone.

I caught Casserman's attention later. 'He ought to be in the hospital,' I said.

Casserman nodded uneasily. 'Yeah. But what can you do? The guy just sits there and won't talk. Just sits and don't even drink his beer anymore.' He shrugged with an uncomfortable air. 'It gives me the jitters.'

I don't know what prompted me to ask the question, but I did. Lowering my voice, I leaned across the bar. 'Is he leaving his dime?'

Casserman shook his head. 'Just forgets, I guess. Hell, I don't care much about *that.* He's been comin' here for years. It's only that he's beginning to get on me nerves a bit.'

Again, the exact sequence of time and events eludes me. But I have the impression that the next evening Fred sat at the far end of the bar as usual. The place was extra busy and I didn't get to talk to Casserman.

I had a late, rush assignment the following night and didn't make it to Casserman's. But the subsequent night I strolled in at the regular time and there sat the runt, pale, silent and really sick looking. His eyes met mine and I nodded. This time, surprisingly, his return nod was actually perceptible. His eyes even held for a few moments and, again, I fancied that I read a mute but desperate and mounting appeal in them.

I was almost impelled to walk to the end of the bar and speak to him, but I didn't. He looked away at the last moment, I hesitated, and the impulse passed. I sat down at my usual place.

A few minutes later, when the tavern had begun to fill up, Casserman leaned across the bar. 'Still not touched his beer. Holy

Jesus! He looks like a walkin' corpse!'

'We ought to do something,' I said.

Casserman shrugged unhappily. 'He don't talk anymore, don't say a word. Maybe before closin' time, you could try to get somethin' out of him?'

I hesitated. 'Yeah. I'll see.'

Although I had been impelled to speak to the runt only a few minutes previously, I now found that my desire to do so had ebbed away. I'm not sure why. Pure selfishness maybe. I suppose I just didn't want to disturb the pleasant aura of late evening which alcohol, companions and a familiar refuge combined to create. Beyond that, I think I felt convinced that the little runt would probably repel my attempts at solicitude with a wall of silence and the whole episode would turn out to be both awkward and embarrassing. In any event, I did nothing.

I suppose my decision to do nothing was the climax. In a sense the business about Fred ended right there, that same evening, no more than a half hour later. I'll try to describe it as I recall it and you can accept or reject it as you see fit.

I can't remember the exact time, right to the minute, but it must have been approximately quarter to, I recollect, clearly, that for some reason I glanced up, toward the end of the bar. Fred was looking at me. His eyes lingered and once more I read a curious, despairing appeal in them. It was so intense and so apparent that it fixed my attention.

I was looking back, still undecided what I should do, when the little runt finally dropped his eyes. A moment later he got up and moved into the men's room, at the rear of the building.

I hesitated for a minute and then acted on impulse. Perhaps, I must have reasoned, if I could speak to the poor little guy in private, he might be willing to talk. Maybe Casserman and I could help him somehow. Get him into a hospital or at least to a doctor.

I got up and walked into the men's room. It was empty.

Let me emphasise two things. First, that I followed the runt into the men's room no more than two minutes after he entered it—actually, I think it was just over a minute. If, in that brief time, he had emerged from the room, lie would have had to open the door, cross my field of vision—I sat staring at the door—and walk the entire length of the bar before leaving by the street entrance. Second, there was absolutely no way out of the men's room except by the single door. There was a small window set in the rear wall, but some years previously someone had smashed through that window and rifled the cash register. Shortly after, Casserman had heavy steel bars set into the window frame. In addition, a thick wire-mesh screen had been placed over the entire window, bars and all, from the outside. Only an insect or a mouse could have gotten through that window without tearing off the wire screen and cutting through at least two or three of the steel bars.

There was a rear door, but it was in the opposite corner of the building, behind the bar. It was bolted and locked and Casserman carried the key. I don't quite know how Casserman passed the fire marshal's annual inspection, but the fact remains it would have been impossible for the runt to leave by that exit unless he went behind the bar and got the key from Casserman—which he did not do.

I stood in that dingy men's room and looked around. The stall doors were attached by springs and they were all wide open. To keep them closed they had to be locked. From the inside. There was no place else in that room where anyone could stand, sit or crouch without being seen.

I walked to the barred window at the rear of the room and gazed out. The bars were in place, the wire screen intact, the window closed and locked.

Only a few yards behind Casserman's place, a series of railroad tracks came together and ran off toward a sprawl of waterfront salt flats. As I stood at the window, frowning in bewilderment, I looked down those empty tracks and for a fleeting second I thought that I saw someone walking along them. I had the odd impression that although this figure was walking slowly, it was, paradoxically, receding rapidly into the distance. Then I decided that my eyes were deceiving me, that a blur of shadows in the moonlight was all that I had actually seen.

As I lingered at the window, looking down that shiny, dwindling road of steel track and wooden ties, a sense of the most indescribable desolation overcame me. I don't possess the words to convey it. A sudden feeling of heart-stopping, overwhelming loneliness washed through me. It was not a mere physical sense of loneliness; it was a lone-liness of the psyche, of the spirit, an abrupt and unaccountable conviction that I was alone and isolated from all humanity, that I was sinking, soul-hungry and desperate, into an awful, inconceivable gulf of immense outer darkness, a universe of unutterable cold, unrelieved and never-ending.

I shuddered and turned away from the window. A minute later I was back at the bar and Casserman came over.

'You see him?' he asked.

I took a long drink and grinned at him rather foolishly. I suppose it was some kind of reaction from the experience I'd just had. 'How could I see him?' I replied. 'He went into the men's room and disappeared!'

Casserman scowled at me. 'I was up near the front; I didn't see him go out.'

I drained my glass and shoved it across the bar. 'Hell, *one* of us needs glasses then!'

I left late, a bit the worse for wear and went home. I didn't sleep well.

The next night when I stopped in at Casserman's, Fred wasn't there. His place at the end of the bar was empty.

When he got a free minute, Casserman came over. 'I'm worried about that little runt. Probably lyin' sick in some flea-bag flophouse.'

I sipped my beer. 'Can you get his address?'

Casserman scratched his head. 'Maybe. Rick Platz used to know all that race-track bunch. Maybe I'll call him tomorrow. No use tonight.'

'By the way,' I said, 'do you know the runt's name—I mean, besides 'Fred?'

Casserman shook his head. 'Cripes. I don't. He just never told me. But Rick probably knows.'

A late assignment kept me from Casserman's the next night. The following evening I stopped in as usual.

Casserman sliced the foam off a beer and set it before me. 'I got the runt's address,' he said with satisfaction. 'Rick didn't know at first but he found out and called me back. Just as I figured, it's a kind of flophouse. Eleven Buren Street, around the corner from Water Street. The runt has a room there. His last name, Rick says, is Amodius.'

'I'll look him up tomorrow,' I promised.

Since I didn't have to report to the city room until four in the afternoon, I had plenty of time the next day. I drove down Water Street, turned at Buren and parked just around the corner in front of a four-storey brick tenement-type building. It was the kind of place which had seen better days fifty years ago. The bricks were black with soot and grime, the window panes cracked and pasted together with tape, the front sidewalk a litter of blown papers and broken bottles.

It was situated in a seedy, waterfront neighborhood and I didn't like leaving my car, but I had little choice.

The doorbell obviously didn't work so I just clumped down a dimly lighted entrance hall until I ran into someone—a wild-looking teenager carrying two gallon jugs.

He shrugged impatiently when I asked for Fred Amodius. 'I dunno no names here. See Mr. Catallo.' He nodded toward a nearby door. I knocked on it.

There was a stir inside and an enormous fat man wearing a satiny pink bathrobe opened the door. He took a swipe at his scattered hair and scowled... 'Yeah?'

When I mentioned Fred Amodius, I saw the blood rising up through his bristly jowls. 'That lousy punk! You're too late, mister! They dragged him out of here yesterday. The lousy punk!'

'He was sick?' I asked.

He grinned evilly. 'Yeah, he was sick all right! So sick he stunk up the place! He musta croaked up there in that closet a coupla weeks ago. The lousy punk! I let him have the place for nothing— over a year now. Said he'd take out the garbage and stuff. Clean up a little. The lousy punk! A month now and he ain't done nothing! Good riddance!'

'Can I see his room?' I asked.

His scowl deepened and he hesitated. Finally he shrugged. 'Sure, if you can stand the stink. Top floor, last room at the back, left. Leave the window open.' He peered at me with suspicion, 'Whatta you lookin' for? You a relative? There's nothin' in the room. That dope didn't leave a dime.'

I told him a distant relative of Amodius had sent me to check the room. He didn't believe me but he let me go up anyway.

I was starting up the stairs when he called out, 'Lousy punk!' I had the feeling, this time, that he meant me instead of Amodius, but I didn't make an issue of it. I supposed he was miffed because I hadn't slipped him a bill.

At the end of the fourth-floor hallway, I saw a tiny door on the left and swung it open. Catallo was right; it was a closet. An undersize cot, a kitchen chair and a wooden box comprised the furniture. The cot was covered with a stained mattress, which looked as if the rats had stampeded in it. The only other things in the room were some newspapers and magazines strewn on the floor and one pair of torn socks tossed in a corner.

The room gave off a sickly-sweetish odour, but it wasn't as bad as I feared. The single window was wide open.

I glanced into the wooden box. It was empty. I closed the door and got out of there.

I reported to Casserman that night. He shook his head, 'I feel bad about it. We waited too long. Maybe we could have done something. But that slob is all wet. The runt wasn't lyin' dead in that room for any two weeks. We saw him here just a few nights ago.'

I sipped my beer thoughtfully. 'Well, Catallo lost track of time, that's all.'

Casserman gave me an enigmatic troubled look and then moved down the bar to wait on a new customer.

I should have dismissed the business from my mind right then and there—I had plenty of other problems to worry about—but I kept fretting about it.

After all, I had detected an odour in the room.

I didn't sleep well that night. The next day I went to see the autopsy surgeon. Not the coroner, but the doctor who had actually performed the autopsy. For the average citizen this might have proved sticky, but a newspaperman does have certain advantages.

I met him in a little anteroom near the morgue, a Doctor Seilman. He was still wearing his white hospital coat but he had taken off his mask and gloves. He nodded.

He remembered the cadaver of the runt, Fred Amodius, very well.

'One of the worst cases of malnourishment I've seen,' he told me. 'He was a walking skeleton.'

'What was the cause of death?' I asked him.

'We put down pneumonia as the immediate cause. But he also had a massive viral infection not necessarily related to the lung condition. Beyond that, he had bleeding ulcers, cirrhosis of the liver and probably a weak heart. Besides the malnutrition.'

'How long had he been dead—before he was found I mean.'

Seilman didn't hesitate. 'Three weeks.'

I stared at him. 'I don't think that's possible.'

He shrugged. 'Well, we don't pretend to pin it right to the day. Three weeks, twenty days, eighteen days, something like that.'

I felt perspiration rolling down my face. 'What, Dr. Seilman, would you say was the absolute minimum?'

He looked at me curiously and thought a minute. 'I'd say the absolute minimum would be sixteen days. There was no evidence of foul play.'

I thanked him and left.

I can't even remember what went on in the city room that night. All I could think about was Catallo's phrase, "croaked up there in that closet a coupla weeks ago". And then Dr. Seilman's "I'd say the absolute minimum would be sixteen days".

It didn't add up. Nothing added up. Because both Casserman and I had seen the runt that last night—and that was only three days before they carried him out of Catallo's closet, less than three full days actually.

I told Casserman that night. He swore. 'Cripes! Somebody's loco! We saw him sittin' there. The both of us can't be crazy!'

'It looks like somebody is,' I said.

He leaned across the bar later in the evening. 'Don't laugh now,' he said frowning, 'but I've been thinkin'. I mean the way the runt didn't drink his beer and stopped leavin' a dime. Could both of us been seein' a ghost?'

I glanced toward the end of the bar. 'Well—could be. But I believe he just kept going longer than they figured anybody could with his ailments. Will power, you know.'

Casserman nodded. 'Yeah, maybe.' He wasn't convinced and neither was I. I kept remembering that sickish-sweet odour up in the closet room.

Even then, I didn't drop the business. I tried to find out all I could about Fred Amodius. There were pitifully few facts available.

Over a period of several weeks I picked up scattered bits of information. Amodius had been an orphan, kicked around from one foster home to another. Sometime in his early teens he had wound up in the street. His formal schooling must have been minimal.

He had wanted to be a jockey but he had never made it—never even came close to it. One rainy day I stood at the big local race track talking to a stable "boy" (he was about sixty).

He picked up a currycomb and shrugged. 'Yeah, I remember the guy, a faded, funny-lookin' little character. Wanted to ride. Everybody just laughed at him. He didn't have nothin'.'

He shook his head. 'He gave up, I guess. Finally tried a stable job, but they kicked him out after a couple days.' He looked up at me. 'You know what, mister?'

'No, what?'

'He frightened the horses! The boss told him "Get lost!" The jerk!'

That's about all I could find out. I suppose there wasn't much more *to* find out. Amodius drifted around the track, panhandled and once in a while picked up some kind of odd job. How he lived as long as he did is a mystery. They put his age down at thirty-four and although there was some uncertainty about it, that must have been fairly close.

He lived in flophouses and cheap hotels, sometimes slept in doorways and wound up in Catallo's miserable little closet room.

So far as I could discover, he had no friends. Women must have been rare, or perhaps non-existent, in his life. One informant told me: 'I never saw that little creep with a dame.' He may have spent some time with a few of the lower-rung prostitutes. There's no way of telling. God knows he didn't have much to offer a woman.

As the stark, pitifully dreary outline of his existence began to take form, I saw why that pale, shadowy, pathetic figure had clung so long to his usual place at the end of Casserman's bar.

He had been an individual with virtually no emotional life. All his years he had known a shabby, bleak and isolated existence. He must have hungered for life, without ever finding it. Hunger, that was the keynote. Hunger, remorseless and unremitting. Hunger for love, for affection, for recognition, for acceptance, for status—for anything.

Having no inner emotional life at all, the thought of being hurled into the detached world of the mind, of spirit, must have been, to him, the ultimate horror. How could he survive in the world not of flesh, he must have subconsciously asked himself, when he had nothing of the spirit to remember?

He must have looked on death, not as release, but as a last unending loneliness. With his inward emptiness, his non-life as it were, his terrible emotional deprivation, he must have neared death with a sense of fearful desperation.

Death loomed before him as an indescribable abyss of enduring darkness, of ultimate isolation.

If we survive death, we survive, probably, on our memories, on our emotional experiences and recollections, on the relationships which enriched our lives.

Amodius had none, or almost none. The outer darkness must have filled him with inconceivable terror.

And that, I think, is why he lingered at Casserman's bar. That is why we saw him there nearly two and a half weeks after he was supposed to be dead. That is why we saw him there, or thought we saw him there, when his cadaver was lying in Catallo's closet.

Casserman's bar was probably the nearest thing to "home" which he had known in many years. If he was not exactly cherished in the establishment, he was certainly not challenged. He was never badgered, nor annoyed, nor made conspicuous. At the worst he was ignored. Casserman himself always treated him courteously; some of the rest of us nodded to him.

I am convinced that some element of him, some residue as it were, anchored itself desperately to Casserman's even after the formal death of the flesh. It clung with inconceivable loneliness and longing to the one spot where it had known a degree of warmth, of toleration, of familiarity and friendliness.

It left with enormous reluctance. It was torn away, I suppose, as the tenuous threads which held it temporarily at last yielded to the irresistible tug of the terrible outer gulfs.

Possibly its terror generated a kind of energy which permitted it to move about in a body which no longer supported life as we normally know it.

But as I recall the shadowy something which I glimpsed receding down the railroad tracks that last night, as I remember the sense of insupportable desolation which swept over me, I think not. I believe the thing which Casserman and I saw on those final nights was sheer spectre.

At least, I am convinced, it was not of this earth.

AUNT HESTER

By Brian Lumley

I SUPPOSE MY AUNT Hester Lang might best be described as the "black sheep" of the family. Certainly no one ever spoke to her, or of her—none of the elders of the family, that is—and if my own little friendship with my aunt had been known I am sure that would have been stamped on too; but of course that friendship was many years ago.

I remember it well: how I used to sneak round to Aunt Hester's house in hoary Castle-Ilden, not far from Harden on the coast, after school when my folks thought I was at Scouts, and Aunt Hester would make me cups of cocoa and we would talk about newts ("efts", she called them), frogs, conkers and other things—things of interest to small boys—until the local Scouts' meeting was due to end, and then I would hurry home.

We (father, mother and myself) left Harden when I was just twelve years old, moving down to London where the Old Man had got himself a good job. I was twenty years old before I got to see my aunt again. In the intervening years I had not sent her so much as a postcard (I've never been much of a letter-writer) and I knew that during the same period of time my parents had neither written nor heard from her; but still that did not stop my mother warning me before I set out for Harden not to "drop in" on Aunt Hester Lang.

No doubt about it, they were frightened of her, my parents—well, if not frightened, certainly they were apprehensive.

Now to me a warning has always been something of a challenge. I had arranged to stay with a friend for a week, a school pal from the good old days, but long before the northbound train stopped at Harden my mind was made up to spend at least a fraction of my time at my aunt's place. Why shouldn't I? Hadn't we always got on famously? Whatever it was she had done to my parents in the past, I could see no good reason why *I* should shun her.

She would be getting on in years a bit now. How old, I wondered? Older than my mother, her sister, by a couple of years—the same age (obviously) as her twin brother, George, in Australia—but of course I was also ignorant of his age. In the end, making what calculations I could, I worked it out that Aunt Hester and her distant brother must have been at least one hundred and eight summers between them. Yes, my aunt must be about fifty-four years old. It was about time someone took an interest in her.

It was a bright Friday night, the first after my arrival in Harden, when the ideal opportunity presented itself for visiting Aunt Hester. My school friend, Albert, had a date—one he did not really want to put off—and though he had tried his best during the day it had early been apparent that his luck was out regards finding, on short notice, a second girl for me. It had been left too late. But in any case, I'm not much on blind dates—and most dates are "blind" unless you really know the girl—and I go even less on doubles; the truth of the matter was that I had wanted the night for my own purposes. And so, when the time came for Albert to set out to meet his girl, I walked off in the opposite direction, across the autumn fences and fields to ancient Castle-Ilden.

I arrived at the little old village at about eight, just as dusk was making its hesitant decision whether or not to allow night's onset, and went straight to Aunt Hester's thatch-roofed bungalow. The place stood (just as I remembered it) at the Blackhill end of cobbled Main Street, in a neat garden framed by cherry trees with the fruit heavy in their branches. As I approached the gate the door opened and out of the house wandered the oddest quartet of strangers I could ever have wished to see.

There was a humped-up, frenetically mobile and babbling old chap, ninety if he was a day; a frumpish fat woman with many quivering chins; a skeletally thin, incredibly tall, ridiculously wrapped-up man in scarf, pencil-slim overcoat, and fur gloves; and finally, a perfectly delicate old lady with a walking-stick and ear-trumpet. They were shepherded by my Aunt Hester, no different it seemed than when I had last seen her, to the gate and out into the street. There followed a piped and grunted hubbub of thanks and general genialities before the four were gone—in the direction of the leaning village pub—leaving my aunt at the gate finally to spot me where I stood in the shadow of one of her cherry trees. She knew me almost at once, despite the interval of nearly a decade.

'Peter?'

'Hello, Aunt Hester.'

'Why, Peter Norton! My favourite young man—and tall as a tree! Come in, come in!'

'It's bad of me to drop in on you like this,' I answered, taking the arm she offered, 'all unannounced and after so long away, but I—'

'No excuses required,' she waved an airy hand before us and smiled up at me, laughter lines showing at the corners of her eyes and in her un-pretty face. 'And you came at just the right time—my group has just left me all alone.'

'Your "group"?'

'My séance group! I've had it for a long time now, many a year. Didn't you know I was a bit on the psychic side? No, I suppose not; your parents wouldn't have told you about *that*, now would they? That's what started it all originally—the trouble in the family, I mean.' We went on into the house.

'Now I had meant to ask you about that,' I told her. 'You mean my parents don't like you messing about with spiritualism? I can see that they wouldn't, of course—not at all the Old Man's cup of tea—but still, I don't really see what it could have to do with them.'

'Not *your* parents, Love,' (she had always called me "Love"), 'mine—and yours later; but especially George, your uncle in Australia. And not just spiritualism, though that has since become part of it. Did you know that my brother left home and settled in Australia because of me?'

A distant look came into her eyes. 'No, of course you didn't, and I don't suppose anyone else would ever have become aware of my power if George hadn't walked me through a window...'

'Eh?' I said, believing my hearing to be out of order. 'Power? Walked you through a window?'

'Yes,' she answered, nodding her head, 'he walked me through a window! Listen, I'll tell you the story from the beginning.'

By that time we had settled ourselves down in front of the fire in Aunt Hester's living room and I was able to scan, as she talked, the paraphernalia her "group" had left behind. There were old leather-bound tomes and treatises, tarot cards, a Ouija board shiny brown with age, oh, and several other items beloved of the spiritualist. I was fascinated, as ever I had been as a boy, by the many obscure curiosities in Aunt Hester's cottage.

'The first I knew of the link between George and myself,' she began, breaking in on my thoughts, 'as apart from the obvious link that exists between all twins, was when we were twelve years old. Your grandparents had taken us, along with your mother, down to the beach at Seaton Carew. It was July and marvellously hot. Well, to cut a long story short, your mother got into trouble in the water.

'She was quite a long way out and the only one anything like close to her was George—who couldn't swim! He'd waded out up to his neck, but he didn't dare go any deeper.

'Now, you can wade a long way out at Seaton. The bottom

shelves off very slowly. George was at least fifty yards out when we heard him yelling that Sis was in trouble...

'At first I panicked and started to run out through the shallow water, shouting to George that he should swim to Sis, which of course he couldn't—*but he did!* Or at least, *I did!* Somehow I'd swapped places with him, do you see? Not physically but mentally. I'd left him behind me in the shallow water, in my body, and I was swimming for all I was worth for Sis in his! I got her back to the shallows with very little trouble—she was only a few inches out of her depth—and then, as soon as the danger was past, I found my consciousness floating back into my own body.

'Well, everyone made a big fuss of George; he was the hero of the day, you see? How had he done it? —they all wanted to know; and all he was able to say was that he'd just seemed to stand there watching himself save Sis. And of course he *had* stood there watching it all—through my eyes!

'I didn't try to explain it; no one would have believed or listened to me anyway, and I didn't really understand it myself—but George was always a bit wary of me from then on. He said nothing, mind you, but I think that even as early as that first time he had an idea...'

Suddenly she looked at me closely, frowning. 'You're not finding all this a bit too hard to swallow, Love?'

'No,' I shook my head. 'Not really. I remember reading somewhere of a similar thing between twins—a sort of Corsican Brothers situation.'

'Oh, but I've heard of many such!' she quickly answered. 'I don't suppose you've read Joachim Feery on the *Necronomicon*?'

'No,' I answered. 'I don't think so.'

'Well, Feery was the illegitimate grandson of Baron Kant, the German "witch-hunter". He died quite mysteriously in 1934 while still a comparatively young man. He wrote a number of occult limited editions—mostly published at his own expense—the vast majority of which religious and other authorities bought up and destroyed as fast as they appeared. Unquestionably—though it has never been discovered where he saw or read them—Feery's source books were very rare and sinister volumes; among them the *Cthaat Aquadingen*, the *Necronomicon*, von Junzt's *Unspeakable Cults*, Prinn's, *De Vermis Mysteriis* and others of that sort. Often Feery's knowledge in respect of such books has seemed almost beyond belief. His quotes, while apparently genuine and authoritative, often differ substantially when compared with the works from which they were supposedly culled. Regarding such discrepancies, Feery claimed that most of his occult knowledge came to him "in dreams"!' She paused, then asked: 'Am I boring you?'

'Not a bit of it,' I answered. 'I'm fascinated.'

'Well, anyhow,' she continued, 'as I've said, Feery must somewhere have seen one of the very rare copies of Abdul Alhazred's *Necronomicon*, in one translation or another, for he published a slim volume of notes concerning that book's contents. I don't own a copy myself but I've read one belonging to a friend of mine, an old member of my group. Alhazred, while being reckoned by many to have been a madman, was without doubt the world's foremost authority on black magic and the horrors of alien dimensions, and he was vastly interested in every facet of freakish phenomena, physical and metaphysical.'

She stood up, went to her bookshelf and opened a large modern volume of Aubrey Beardsley's fascinating drawings, taking out a number of loose white sheets bearing lines of her own neat handwriting.

'I've copied some of Feery's quotes, supposedly from Alhazred. Listen to this one:

"Tis a veritable & attestable Fact, that

between certain related Persons there exists a Bond more powerful than the strongest Ties of Flesh & Family, whereby one such Person may be *aware* of all the Trials & Pleasures of the other, yea, even to experiencing the Pains or Passions of one far distant; & further, there are those whose skills in such Matters are aided by forbidden Knowledge or Intercourse through dark Magic with Spirits & Beings of outside Spheres. Of the latter: I have sought them out, both Men & Women, & upon Examination have in all Cases discovered them to be Users of Divination, Observers of Times, Enchanters, Witches, Charmers, or Necromancers. All claimed to work their Wonders through Intercourse with dead & de-parted Spirits, but I fear that often such Spirits were evil Angels, the Messengers of the Dark One & yet more ancient Evils. Indeed, among them were some whose Powers were prodigious, who might at will *inhabit* the Body of another even at a great distance & against the Will & often unbeknown to the Sufferer of such Outrage..."

She put down the papers, sat back and looked at me quizzically.

'That's all very interesting,' I said after a moment, 'but hardly applicable to yourself.'

'Oh, but it is, Love,' she protested. 'I'm George's twin, for one thing, and for another—'

'But you're no witch or necromancer!'

'No, I wouldn't say so—but I am a "User of Divinations", and I do "work my Wonders through Intercourse with dead & departed Spirits". That's what spiritualism is all about.'

'You mean you actually take this, er, Alhazred and spiritualism and all seriously?' I deprecated.

She frowned. 'No, not Alhazred, not really,' she answered after a moment's thought. 'But he is interesting, as you said. As for spiritualism: yes, I *do* take it seriously. Why, you'd be amazed at some of the vibrations I've been getting these last three weeks or so. *Very* disturbing, but so far rather incoherent; frantic, in fact. I'll track him down eventually, though—the spirit, I mean...'

We sat quietly then, contemplatively for a minute or two. Frankly, I didn't quite know what to say; but then she went on: 'Anyway, we were talking about George and how I believed that even after that first occasion he had a bit of an idea that I was at the root of the thing. Yes, I really think he did. He said nothing, and yet...

'And that's not all, either. It was some time after that day on the beach before Sis could be convinced that she hadn't been saved by me. She was sure it had been me, not George, who pulled her out of the deep water.

'Well, a year or two went by, and school-leaving exams came up. I was all right, a reasonable scholar—I had always been a bookish kid—but poor old George...' She shook her head sadly. My uncle, it appeared, had not been too bright.

After a moment she continued. 'Dates were set for the exams and two sets of papers were prepared, one for the boys, another for the girls. I had no trouble with my paper, I knew even before the results were announced that I was through easily—but before that came George's turn. He'd been worrying and chewing, cramming for all he was worth, biting his nails down to the elbows... and getting nowhere. I was in bed with flu when the day of his exams came round, and I remember how I just lay there fretting over him.

He was my brother, after all.

'I must have been thinking of him just a bit too hard, though, for before I knew it there I was, staring down hard at an exam paper, sitting in a class full of boys in the old school!

'...An hour later I had the papers all finished, and then I concentrated myself back home again. This time it was a definite effort for me to find my way back to my own body.

'The house was in an uproar. I was downstairs in my dressing-gown; mother had an arm round me and was trying to console me; father was yelling and waving his arms about like a lunatic. "The girl's gone *mad!*" I remember him exploding, red faced and a bit frightened.

'Apparently I had rushed downstairs about an hour earlier. I had been shouting and screaming tearfully that I'd miss the exam, and I had wanted to know what I was doing home. And when they had called me *Hester* instead *of George!* Well, then I had seemed to go completely out of my mind!

'Of course, I had been feverish with flu for a couple of days. That was obviously the answer: I had suddenly reached the height of a hitherto unrecognized delirious fever, and now the fever had broken I was going to be all right. That was what they said...

'George eventually came home with his eyes all wide and staring, frightened-looking, and he stayed that way for a couple of days. He avoided me like the plague! But the next week—when it came out about how good his marks were, how easily he had passed his examination papers—well...'

'But surely he must have known,' I broke in. What few doubts I had entertained were now gone forever. She was plainly not making all of this up.

'But why should he have known, Love? He knew he'd had two pretty nightmarish experiences, sure enough, and that somehow they had been connected with me; but he couldn't possibly know that they had their origin in me—that I formed their focus.'

'He did find out, though?'

'Oh, yes, he did,' she slowly answered, her eyes seeming to glisten just a little in the homely evening glow of the room. 'And as I've said, that's why he left home in the end. It happened like this:

'I had never been a pretty girl—no, don't say anything, Love. You weren't even a twinkle in your father's eye then, he was only a boy himself, and so you wouldn't know. But at a time of life when most girls only have to pout to set the boys on fire, well, I was only very plain—and I'm probably giving myself the benefit of the doubt at that.

'Anyway, when George was out nights—walking his latest girl, dancing, or whatever—I was always at home on my own with my books. Quite simply, I came to be terribly jealous of my brother. Of course, you don't know him, he had already been gone something like fifteen years when you were born, but George was a handsome lad. Not strong, mind you, but long and lean and a natural for the girls.

'Eventually he found himself a special girlfriend and came to spend all his time with her. I remember being furious because he wouldn't tell me anything about her...'

She paused and looked at me and after a while I said:

'Uhhuh?' inviting her to go on.

'It was one Saturday night in the spring, I remember, not long after our nineteenth birthday, and George had spent the better part of an hour dandying himself up for this unknown girl. That night he seemed to take a sort of stupid, well, *delight* in spiting me; he refused to answer my questions about his girl or even mention her name. Finally, after he had set his tie straight and slicked his hair down for what seemed like the thousandth time, he dared to wink at me—maliciously, I thought, in my jealousy—as he went out into the night.

'That did it. Something *snapped!* I stamped my foot and rushed upstairs to my room for a good cry. And in the middle of crying I had my idea—'

'You decided to, er, swap identities with your brother, to have a look at his girl for yourself,' I broke in. 'Am I right?'

She nodded in answer, staring at the fire; ashamed of herself, I thought, after all this time. 'Yes, I did,' she said.

'For the first time I used my power for my own ends. And mean and despicable ends they were.

'But this time it wasn't like before. There was no in-stantaneous, involuntary flowing of my psyche, as it were. No immediate change of personality. I had to force it, to concentrate and concentrate and *push* myself. But in a short period of time, before I even knew it, well, there I was.'

'There you were? In Uncle George's body?'

'Yes, in his body, looking out through his eyes, holding in his hand the cool, slender hand of a very pretty girl. I had expected the girl, of course, and yet...

'Confused and blustering, letting go of her hand, I jumped back and bumped into a man standing behind me.

'The girl was saying: "George, what's wrong?" in a whisper, and people were staring. We were in a second-show picture-house queue. Finally I managed to mumble an answer, in a horribly hoarse, unfamiliar, frightened voice—George's voice, obviously, and my fear—and then the girl moved closer and kissed me gently on the cheek!

'She did! But of course she would, wouldn't she, if I were George? "Why, you jumped then like you'd been stung—" she started to say; but I wasn't listening, Peter, for I had jumped again, even more violently, shrinking away from her in a kind of horror. I must have gone crimson, standing there in that queue, with all those unfamiliar people looking at me—*and I had just been kissed by a girl!*

'You see, I wasn't thinking like George at all! I just wished with all my heart that I hadn't interfered, and before I knew it I had George's body in motion and was running down the road, the picture-house queue behind me and the voice of this sweet little girl echoing after me in pained and astonished disbelief.

'Altogether my spiteful adventure had taken only a few minutes, and, when at last I was able to do so, I controlled myself—or rather, George's self—and hid in a shop doorway. It took another minute or two before I was composed sufficiently to manage a, well, a "return trip", but at last I made it and there I was back in my room.

'I had been gone no more than seven or eight minutes all told, but I wasn't back to *exactly* where I started out from. Oh, George hadn't gone rushing downstairs again in a hysterical fit, like that time when I sat his exam for him—though of course the period of *transition* had been a much longer one on that occasion—but he had at least moved off the bed. I found myself standing beside the window...' She paused.

'And afterwards?' I prompted her, fascinated.

'Afterwards?' she echoed me, considering it. 'Well, George was very quiet about it... No, that's not quite true. It's not that he was quiet, rather that he avoided me more than ever, to such an extent that I hardly ever saw him—no more than a glimpse at a time as he came and went. Mother and father didn't notice George's increased coolness towards me, but I certainly did. I'm pretty sure it was then that he had finally recognized the source of this thing that came at odd times like some short-lived insanity to plague him. Yes, and looking back, I can see how I might easily have driven George completely insane! But of course, from that time on he was forewarned...'

'Forewarned?' I repeated her. 'And the next time he—'

'The next time?' She turned her face so that I could see the fine scars on her otherwise smooth left cheek. I had always wondered about those scars. 'I don't remember a great deal about the next time—shock, I suppose, a "mental block", you might call it—but anyway, the next time was the *last* time!

'There was a boy who took me out once or twice, and I remember that when he stopped calling for me it was because of something George had said to him. Six months had gone by since my shameful and abortive experiment, and now I deliberately put it out of my mind as I determined to teach George a lesson. You must understand, Love, that this boy I mentioned, well... he meant a great deal to me.

'Anyway, I was out to get my own back. I didn't know how George had managed to make it up with his girl, but he had. I was going to put an end to their little romance once and for all.

'It was a fairly warm, early October, I remember, when my chance eventually came. A Sunday afternoon, and George was out walking with his girl. I had it planned minutely. I knew exactly what I must say, how I must act, what I must do. I could do it in two minutes flat, and be back in my own body before George knew what was going on. For the first time my intentions were *deliberately* malicious...'

I waited for my aunt to continue, and after a while again prompted her: 'And? Was this when—'

'Yes, this was when he walked me through the window. Well, he didn't exactly walk me through it—I believe I leapt; or rather, he leapt me, if you see what I mean. One minute I was sitting on a grassy bank with the same sweet little girl... and the next there was this awful pain—my whole body hurt, and it was *my* body, for my consciousness was suddenly back where it belonged. Instantaneously, inadvertently, I was—myself!

'But I was lying crumpled on the lawn in front of the house! I remember

107

seeing splinters of broken glass and bits of yellow-painted wood from my shattered bedroom window, and then I went into a faint with the pain.

'George came to see me in the hospital—once. He sneered when my parents had their backs turned. He leaned over my bed and said: '*Got* you, Hester!' Just that, nothing more.

'I had a broken leg and collarbone. It was three weeks before they let me go home. By then George had joined the Merchant Navy and my parents knew that somehow I was to blame. They were never the same to me from that time on. George had been the Apple of the Family Eye, if you know what I mean. They knew that his going away, in some unknown way, had been my fault. I did have a letter from George—well, a note. It simply warned me "never to do it again", that there were worse things than falling through windows!'

'And you never did, er, do it again?'

'No, I didn't dare; I haven't dared since. There *are* worse things, Love, than being walked through a window! And if George hates me still as much as he might...

'But I've often *wanted* to do it again. George has two children, you know?'

I nodded an affirmation: 'Yes, I've heard mother mention them. Joe and Doreen?'

'That's right,' she nodded. 'They're hardly children any more, but I think of them that way. They'll be in their twenties now, your cousins. George's wife wrote to me once many years ago. I've no idea how she got my address. She did it behind George's back, I imagine. Said how sorry she was that there was "trouble in the family". She sent me photographs of the kids. They were beautiful. For all I know there may have been other children later—even grandchildren.'

'I don't think so,' I told her. 'I think I would have known.

They're still pretty reserved, my folks, but I would have learned that much, I'm sure. But tell me: how is it that you and mother aren't closer? I mean, she never talks about you, my mother, and yet you are her sister.'

'Your mother is two years younger than George and me,' my aunt informed me. 'She went to live with her grandparents down South when she was thirteen. Sis, you see, was the brilliant one. George was a bit dim; I was clever enough; but Sis, she was really clever. Our parents sent Sis off to live with Granny, where she could attend a school worthy of her intelligence. She stayed with Gran from then on. We simply drifted apart...

'Mind you, we'd never been what you might call close, not for sisters. Anyhow, we didn't come together again until she married and came back up here to live, by which time George must have written to her and told her one or two things. I don't know what or how much he told her, but—well, she never bothered with me—and anyway I was working by then and had a flat of my own.

'Years passed, I hardly ever saw Sis, her little boy came along—you, Love—I fell in with a spiritualist group, making real friends for the first time in my life; and, well, that was that. My interest in spiritualism, various other ways of mine that didn't quite fit the accepted pattern, the unspoken thing I had done to George... we drifted apart. You understand?'

I nodded. I felt sorry for her, but of course I could not say so. Instead I laughed awkwardly and shrugged my shoulders. 'Who needs people?'

She looked shocked. 'We all do, Love!' Then for a while she was quiet, staring into the fire.

'I'll make a brew of tea,' she suddenly said, then looked at me and smiled in a fashion I well remembered. 'Or should we have cocoa?'

'Cocoa!' I instinctively laughed, relieved at the change of

subject.

She went into the kitchen and I lit a cigarette. Idle, for the moment, I looked about me, taking up the loose sheets of paper that Aunt Hester had left on her occasional table. I saw at once that many of her jottings were concerned with extracts from exotic books. I passed over the piece she had read out to me and glanced at another sheet. Immediately my interest was caught; the three passages were all from the Holy Bible:

> "Regard not them that have familiar spirits, neither seek after wizards, to be defiled by them." Lev. 19:31.

> "Then said Saul unto his servants, Seek me a woman that hath a familiar spirit, that I may go to her and enquire of her. And his servants said to him, Behold, there is a woman that hath a familiar spirit at En-dor." I Sam. 28:6,7.

> "Many of them also which used curious arts brought their books together, and burned them before all men." Acts 19.19.

The third sheet contained a quote from *Today's Christian:*

> "To dabble in matters such as these is to reach within demoniac circles, and it is by no means rare to discover scorn and scepticism transformed to hysterical possession in persons whose curiosity has led them merely to attend so-called 'spiritual séances'. These things of which I speak are of a nature as serious as any in

the world today, and I am only one among many to utter a solemn warning against any inter- course with 'spirit forces' or the like, whereby the unutterable evil of demonic possession could well be the horrific outcome."

Finally, before she returned with a steaming jug of cocoa and two mugs, I read another of Aunt Hester's extracts, this one again from Feery's *Notes on the Necronomicon:*

> "Yea, & I discovered how one might, be he an Adept & his familiar Spirits powerful enough, control the Wanderings or Migration of his Essence into all manner of Beings & Person— even from beyond the Grave of Sod or the Door of the Stone Sepulchre..."

I was still pondering this last extract an hour later, as I walked Harden's night streets towards my lodgings at the home of my friend.

Three evenings later, when by arrangement I returned to my aunt's cottage in old Castle-Ilden, she was nervously waiting for me at the gate and whisked me breathlessly inside. She sat me down, seated herself opposite and clasped her hands in her lap almost in the attitude of an excited young girl.

'Peter, Love, I've had an idea—such a simple idea that it amazes me I never thought of it before.'

'An idea? How do you mean, Aunt Hester—what sort of idea? Does it involve me?'

'Yes, I'd rather it were you than any other. After all, you know the story now...'

I frowned as an oddly foreboding shadow darkened latent areas of my consciousness. Her words had been innocuous enough as of yet, and there seemed no reason why I should suddenly feel so— *uncomfortable*, but—

'The story?' I finally repeated her. 'You mean this idea of yours concerns—Uncle George?'

'Yes, I do!' she answered. 'Oh, Love, I can see them; if only for a brief moment or two, I can see my nephew and niece. You'll help me? I know you will.'

The shadow thickened darkly, growing in me, spreading from hidden to more truly conscious regions of my mind. 'Help you? You mean you intend to—' I paused, then started to speak again as I saw for sure what she was getting at and realized that she meant it: 'But haven't you said that this stuff was too dangerous? The last time you—'

'Oh, yes, I know,' she impatiently argued, cutting me off. 'But now, well, it's different. I won't stay more than a moment or two— just long enough to see the children—and then I'll get straight back... *here*. And there'll be precautions. It can't fail, you'll see.'

'Precautions?' Despite myself I was interested.

'Yes,' she began to talk faster, growing more excited with each passing moment. 'The way I've worked it out, it's perfectly safe. To start with, George will be asleep—he won't know anything about it. When his sleeping mind moves into my body, why, it will simply stay asleep! On the other hand, when *my* mind moves into *his* body, then I'll be able to move about and—'

'And use your brother as a keyhole!' I blurted, surprising even myself. She frowned, then turned her face away. What she planned was wrong. I knew it and so did she, but if my outburst had shamed her it certainly had not deterred her—not for long.

When she looked at me again her eyes were almost pleading. 'I know how it must look to you, Love, but it's not so. And I know that I must seem to be a selfish woman, but that's not quite true either. Isn't it natural that I should want to see my family? They are mine, you know. George, my brother; his wife, my sister-in-law; their children, my nephew and niece. Just a—yes—a "peep", if that's the way you see it. But, Love, I *need* that peep. I'll only have a few moments, and I'll have to make them last me for the rest of my life.'

I began to weaken. 'How will you go about it?'

'First, a glance,' she eagerly answered, again reminding me of a young girl. 'Nothing more, a mere glance. Even if he's awake he won't ever know I was there; he'll think his mind wandered for the merest second. If he *is* asleep, though, then I'll be able to, well, "wake him up", see his wife—and, if the children are still at home, why, I'll be able to see them too. Just a glance.'

'But suppose something does go wrong?' I asked bluntly, coming back to earth 'Why, you might come back and find your head in the gas oven! What's to stop him from slashing your wrists? That only takes a second, you know.'

'That's where you come in, Love.' She stood up and patted me on the cheek, smiling cleverly...' You'll be right here to see that nothing goes wrong.'

'But—'

'And to be doubly sure,' she cut me off, 'why, *I'll be tied in my chair!* You can't walk through windows when tied down, now can you?'

Half an hour later, still suffering inwardly from that as yet unspecified foreboding, I had done as Aunt Hester directed me to do, tying her wrists to the arms of her cane chair with soft but fairly strong bandages from her medicine cabinet in the bathroom.

She had it all worked out, reasoning that it would be very early morning in Australia and that her brother would still be sleeping. As soon as she was comfortable, without another word, she closed her eyes and let her head fall slowly forward onto her chest. Outside, the sun still had some way to go to setting; inside, the room was still warm—yet I shuddered oddly with a deep, nervous chilling of my blood.

It was then that I tried to bring the thing to a halt, calling her name and shaking her shoulder, but she only brushed my hand away and hushed me. I went back to my chair and watched her anxiously.

As the shadows seemed visibly to lengthen in the room and my skin cooled, her head sank even deeper onto her chest, so that I began to think she had fallen asleep.

Then she settled herself more comfortably yet and I saw that she was still awake, merely preparing her body for her brother's slumbering mind.

In another moment I knew that something had changed.

Her position was as it had been; the shadows crept slowly still; the ancient clock on the wall ticked its regular chronological message; but I had grown inexplicably colder, and there was this feeling that, *something* had changed...

Suddenly there flashed before my mind's eye certain of those warning jottings I had read only a few nights earlier, and there and then I was determined that this thing should go no further. Oh, she had warned me not to do anything to frighten or disturb her, but this was different. Somehow I knew that if I didn't act now—

'Hester! Aunt Hester!' I jumped up and moved toward her, my throat dry and my words cracked and unnatural-sounding. And she lifted her head and opened her eyes.

For a moment I thought that everything was all right—then...

She cried out and stood up, ripped bandages falling in tatters from strangely strong wrists. She mouthed again, staggering and patently disorientated. I fell back in dumb horror, knowing that something was very wrong and yet unable to put my finger on the trouble.

My aunt's eyes were wide now and bulging, and for the first time she seemed to see me, stumbling toward me with slack jaw and tongue protruding horribly between long teeth and drawn-back lips. It was then that I knew what was wrong, that this frightful *thing* before me was not my aunt, and I was driven backward before its stumbling approach, warding it off with waving arms and barely articulate cries.

Finally, stumbling more frenziedly now, clawing at empty air inches in front of my face, she—it—spoke: 'No !' the awful voice gurgled over its wriggling tongue. 'No, Hester, you... you *fool!* I warned you...'

And in that same instant I saw not an old woman, *but the horribly alien figure of a man in a woman's form!*

More grotesque than any drag artist, the thing pirouetted in grim, constricting agony, its strange eyes glazing even as I stared in a paralysis of horror. Then it was all over and the frail scarecrow of flesh, purple tongue still protruding from frothing lips, fell in a crumpled heap to the floor.

That's it, that's the story—not a tale I've told before, for there would have been too many questions, and it's more than possible that my version would not be believed. Let's face it, who *would* believe me? No, I realized this as soon as the thing was done, and so I simply got rid of the torn bandages and called in a doctor. Aunt Hester died of a heart attack, or so I'm told, and perhaps she did—straining to do that which, even with her powers, should never have been possible.

During this last fortnight or so since it happened, I've been trying to convince myself that the doctor was right (which I was quite willing enough to believe at the time), but I've been telling myself lies. I think I've known the real truth ever since my parents got the letter from Australia. And lately, reinforcing that truth, there have been the dreams and the daydreams—*or are they?*

This morning I woke up to a lightless void—a numb, black, silent void—wherein I was incapable of even the smallest movement, and I was horribly, hideously frightened. It lasted for only a moment, that's all, but in that moment it seemed to me that I was dead—or that the living *me* inhabited a dead body!

Again and again I find myself thinking back on the mad Arab's words as reported by Joachim Feery : "...even from beyond the Grave of Sod..." And in the end I know that this is indeed the answer.

That is why I'm flying tomorrow to Australia. Ostensibly I'm visiting my uncle's wife, my Australian aunt; but really I'm only interested in him, in Uncle George himself. I don't know what I'll be able to do, or even if there is anything I *can* do. My efforts may well be completely useless, and yet I must try to do something.

I *must* try, for I know now that it's that or find myself once again, perhaps permanently, locked in that hellish, nighted—place?—of black oblivion and insensate silence. In the dead and rotting body of my Uncle George, already buried three weeks when Aunt Hester put her mind in his body—*the body she's now trying to vacate in favour of mine!*

A PENTAGRAM FOR CENAIDE

By Eddy C. Bertin

JACK MORGAN WAS a painter, or at least that was what he always said, and his close friends—those whose judgment he cared about—agreed with him on that point, so it hardly mattered what the critics said about his work, whenever they did take the trouble to say something. His life had always been a very calm and peaceful one, he liked drinking, but not much more than anyone else, and he had tried a few mild drugs too, and had stayed away from them after a severe headache. He had an exceptional ear for music, and always claimed that he could get high on hearing music, so why spend hard cash for ersatz? He had known, and loved, and hated a few women in. his life, and had left them all behind, or they had left him behind depending on what viewpoint one takes. Time had come for a marriage, which never realized, and time had gone past that point too. Jack also liked laughing, and simple fun as well as enjoy reading Sartre. He had many friends who liked him very much until he needed them, when they always seemed to be just out of reach, but always eager to return when he didn't need, or didn't want their help anymore.

He read a lot, from crime novels to Wodehouse, and from the classics to science-fiction, and had a healthy distaste for ladies' novels, until he fell right into one himself, and gradually discovered that there was no way out. The newly arisen dilemma, which had been there for a long time already if he had only seen it, embittered him at first, and angered him. It came in the way of his work, and in his own way he was a straightforward man who hated dilemmas, which couldn't be solved, but he also prided himself in this fact, and that was what made him unable to solve his particular predicament. That was when he discovered, surprising himself most of all, that he was in love with his best friend's wife.

Paul and his wife Cenaide were long time friends of Jack, who used to drop in on him at the weirdest hours of day and night, and he was always ready for them, for a drink, and a chat; besides, he used to visit them quite a lot himself. Cenaide wasn't exactly a classic beauty, and neither was she a very intelligent woman, but one evening when they had gone to a dance, the three of them, and he took her in his arms, felt the softness of her cheek and the tickling of her hair against his face, the suppleness of her body against his, he suddenly realized that he loved her. He had known love before, and he still remembered how it felt and tasted and then hurt afterwards, so this surprised him, then he found it rather funny, and then it angered him. He had no business being in love with this girl, he told himself. Her hair was too short, he had always liked long hair, and the colour wasn't right either. Her manner of speech was rude and she spoke with a strong cheap dialect, which she never was able to hide. No doubt she had lots of personal, annoying habits, and she couldn't even talk about things on his own level of understanding. Above all she was married to his friend, whom she loved very much, of that he was certain. But he loved her with a sudden furious passion, which must have been smoldering in the depths of his mind for some time already, unnoticed. When he began thinking seriously about it later, when he was alone in his room, he recalled the fun they had had just by being together, talking about a lot of stupid unimportant things. He began to remember the peace he had felt, just sitting there and talking to her, knowing that she was near. He began to recall many things, small silly things, but they all added up as he brought them out of their hiding places in his mind, the tingle in his fingers when he touched her hand as she passed him his drink, and the warmth he had felt one evening when she had drunk a few glasses too much of the bottle of wine he had brought with him and had fallen asleep on the couch, and he had looked down upon her relaxed, resting face. He remembered now the sudden flare of anger he had felt one day when Paul had been shouting at her for some unimportant stupidity, and his uneasiness when he had visited them one evening, and she hadn't been home, arriving very late.

He tried the shortest way out of this silly situation, and stopped visiting them without giving a reason, but they came to him, bewildered, and he never let someone stand before a closed door. He tried to be rude, and only succeeded in surprising and hurting them, but they came back nevertheless, and he couldn't keep on being rude to *her*. Then the pain began, and the uneasiness, standing before his window in his empty room, looking out over the rain-shrouded city roofs, smoking a cigarette, the smoke biting in his eyes. He took to taking solitary walks through the empty night streets, alone with his brooding thoughts, and this insane love for a woman who wasn't his, and who would never be his. But the darkness never gives an answer, and if there were an answer to it, it would have to come out of himself.

He couldn't work anymore with the accuracy so typical for his fingers, starting three paintings, leaving the first one unfinished, tearing the second apart with his knife, and throwing the third against the wall with such a force that it split. He tried looking at it logically, but refused to come into agreement with himself. At first he viewed it as a friendship's dilemma, until he discovered that he couldn't care less. He knew how his friend felt about his wife, a superficial love which had drifted into habit through the years. Paul was no real obstacle, Jack wouldn't stop because of him. But the real barrier was lying inside Jack himself, and in his guesswork concerning her feelings. He knew for certain that she cared for him only as a good friend, and nothing more, and there wasn't the slightest chance of a step out of line, because her narrow mindedness on such matters had often before surprised him. Especially as he knew that Paul was far from a faithful husband, and sometimes it was so eye piercing that it seemed almost impossible for Cenaide not to notice it. She didn't however, or else plainly refused to see things in their true light. She cared a lot for her husband, and would never let him go. Along those lines she also didn't give a damn for Jack Morgan.

As time passed, Jack's mind slowly turned into a chaotic labyrinth through which he walked without Ariadne's thread; there were nights when he drank too much just trying to set his mind at peace and have a clear look at things, because contrary to most people, an intoxicated state sometimes did give him a better insight into himself and other people's behaviour; but not this time. Reality was turning into a nightmare, his thoughts swarmed through his skull as dark night moths, he couldn't grasp them or bring any order in them, they kept on escaping him, leaving him in his confusion. They went out together more often, but though he danced many times with the girl, there never was a real contact between them though their bodies touched. Her back always seemed rigid against his hands as a strained spring; her goodnight kisses cold, hurried and impersonal.

He often desperately thought of simply telling her he loved her, but he didn't dare risk their friendship. He was practically certain that she'd refuse him, maybe even be horrified at his feelings, and in any case he would never see her again then. He couldn't risk that, but neither was he able to reject his own feelings. Of course there were always other ways out, but Jack didn't want to take those. He had never been a violent man, and murder just didn't appeal to him. Not counting the fact that it would all have to be worked out in elaborate detail and executed in cold blood, some-thing which he wasn't sure he was capable of, there was always the chance that Cenaide was one of that type of women who prefers to remain a suffering widow for the rest of her life. So Jack tried the other way out.

He had always been fascinated by the strange and the occult, and a long set of tomes on witchcraft and sorcery was among his books. For fun they had even once tried to hold a séance, but except for the nuisance of a poltergeist—all too clearly created by Paul's knee below the table—they hadn't been able to get any results. So the group had discarded the supernatural, but it had kept on fascinating Jack. He didn't exactly believe in the "supernatural" in the popular sense of the word, and he still thought that the general uprising of interest in the so-called "old sciences", in astrology, spiritualism and erotic orgies poorly disguised as witchcraft were mainly a reaction against the materialistic world image, a protest against the real sciences which were being blamed for the kind of world we live in. He knew a few practising witches, and even a medium of two, and he realized that some of them at least really believed in what they were doing. Their belief was genuine... but were the results? Some of them seemed to be, but were they really brought forth by something from the beyond, or was there a more materialistic origin to be found? Jack refused to believe in a heaven and hell, and in a horned and tailed Satan, but he did believe in the human mind, and in its unused potential. He believed in elemental forces, existing in nature since the beginning of time and only waiting to be discovered, elemental forms of energy of which we are yet unaware, and which can sometimes manifest them-selves as an "evil" or a "good" force, not because they are good or evil, but because of the way they are invoked and used. It seemed much more likely and logical than imagining some "beyond" where bodiless spirits are eternally imprisoned, waiting from some rich and bored idiots to start playing with fake spiritualism, just to get a few silly messages.

Now it stopped being a pastime, and Jack began studying the occult in dead seriousness. He started by discarding the general works on magic, and began searching for the rare books, the real books that had not been written with a sensation-hungry public of laymen in mind. What he needed were works written by people who really knew what they were doing. He spent a lot of money, and quite some time hunting them down, but obtain them he did, and study them, through the lonely hours of dark nights, while slow rain drizzled down from a leaden sky. He didn't paint often anymore, there was no time for that, but he kept on seeing Paul and Cenaide, though every second he was close to her hurt him, and every evening after they had separated there was an empty hollowness in his brain.

Then, when he thought he knew enough, and he had obtained all he would need, he drew a pentagram for Cenaide.

First he took an empty canvas, and drew the pentagram on it, with strong strokes of black paint. Then he drew the bigger pentagram on the floor of his study, placing the canvas in the center of it. He made the five marks on the corners, and wrote the formulas, feeling silly all the time. It was the only way, however, he had found of making direct contact with the elemental forces, no matter what form they would take. Much of it was maybe folkloristic and unnecessary for his means, but there was no way to *find* out what was really needed and what not, except by trying it out. Then he spoke the spells, reciting the difficult words in a soft sing-song voice, and burned the needed ingredients inside the pentagram.

Something came.

Or maybe some "things" came, he couldn't be sure, except that whatever they were, they were certainly not of this earth. They moved slowly, almost crawling through the darkness which filled the room; and though he sometimes thought something here or there looked vaguely human, he never could be sure, and probably it was his own mind which made it resemble something familiar. He didn't try to speak to them, for he didn't think they were really intelligent, or even alive in the strictest sense of the word. They were forces, pure energy, but somehow managed to spread an aura around them which he could only define as purely evil, though this couldn't really be so. He had prepared himself well however, and slowly began doing what had to be done, putting his own will on the free energy-things, chanting the old words and making the old gestures with his hands. It took a long time, and when he finally released them, and the moving darkness lifted from the room, he was soaked with sweat. The pentagram on the canvas however was no longer black, it was silvery white, and seemed to be pulsating with a strange life of its own. He stood looking at it for a long time, then got his brush and began painting the canvas in grey, until the pentagram was covered completely.

The next day he visited Paul and Cenaide, declared that he had been commissioned for a group of paintings for a future exhibition, and asked Cenaide if she wanted to pose for him. He wanted to try some new ideas, and had decided to stick to portraits for a few paintings at least. She was surprised and flattered of course, and agreed immediately. So the evenings of the next weeks—because she had her daytime job to attend to—were spent in bringing the face, that not so very special face he loved so much, on the grey-covered canvas. He began by sketching her face on the uniform background, as she was posing rather awkwardly. Then he began filling in the background, making it an old wooden table of a country inn, in which she was sitting, looking straightforward. These evenings were heaven for Jack, as she was with him almost all of the time, and as he was painting he drank in her beauty. Sometimes Paul came along also, changing the records on the gramophone, and for the rest just sitting there, watching. But it wasn't quite as it had to be, there was a strange repellant sensation when he was really close to her, almost as if they were two negative poles rejecting each other. Even when they went out for relaxation, they didn't seem as close as before. He didn't sleep easily anymore, it was as if the dark took strange and alien shapes around him, which were always there, mocking him. Weird things began to visit his dreams, and gibbered to him in unearthly tongues which he couldn't understand, so that he awoke having the impression of not having slept at all, to the contrary, he felt abominably tired.

Then he discovered that it didn't work. Maybe he didn't know as much about magic as he thought, or he had done something wrong, but the power of the pentagram didn't work. The unseen distance between him and Cenaide seemed to be growing, almost as if something was constantly interfering. Anger and bitterness came, and finally, acceptance.

The acceptance was the hardest of all, because it felt as if he was cutting away part of himself, accepting the cold fact that she would never love him. He couldn't think clearly for some time, it dampened the lights around him, took away the beauty of music, seemed to cover the paintings on his walls with greyness.

Then he began concentrating on the portrait. If he couldn't have her, he could give to her. The portrait became an obsession, just as the girl had been, as he transferred all his feelings onto the canvas. He made the painted blue eyes cry for him, made the small fresh mouth without traces of lipstick smile for him. He put it all in the portrait, all the months of yearning, the nights of waking, the tears he had never cried, he gave them flesh and blood in his portrait. He was no longer painting a woman, he was painting the image of love, the essence of the phenomena of love, not sexual attraction or desire, and not intellectual contact or sympathy or pity, but the very spirit of unexplainable love, without thinking, without conditions. He painted it with the colours of hope and yet of sadness, with bitterness and melancholy, with dreams and night-mares. The same nightmares which swam through his mind at night, when he was tossing on his bed, trying to get some sleep, and also trying to shut the living darkness out of his sight.

Finally the painting was completed, and he asked them to come over in the evening and see the finished product. That day he corrected the last minuscule details, a final line here, a last shade of paint there, and all the time the air itself around him seemed to be alive, full of strange moving things, which he couldn't see and couldn't understand. Sometimes he feared he was going insane.

They couldn't speak when they saw the portrait, that evening. Cenaide said in a hushed voice that it was... beautiful, more beautiful than any face she had ever seen, and surely this couldn't be HER face he had painted? Of course it was her own face, and it had to be beautiful, but for the first time she was seeing herself as Jack saw her, covering all mediocrity with the radiant colour of love, which he would never see on her real features.

He laughed at their sincere admiration, and listened to them proclaiming a great future for him as a portrait painter, knowing that he would never be able to do it again. They had brought a few bottles, which were opened and emptied, and there was a lot of joking and small talk before they finally left.

After they had gone, he locked the door carefully behind them, then turned and confronted the picture. The eyes of the painting seemed to be following any movement he made. 'Now, at last, we're alone, my love,' he whispered softly.

Again he drew the big pentagram on the floor of his room, then placed the painting in the centre of it. He lit the five strangely wrought candles at the five corners of the star, and burned the ingredients he had prepared. A strange but not exactly disagree-able odour began to spread through the room. Darkness came, not gradually as when evening falls, because it was night outside aleady, but sharply; an alien darkness which began seeping down from the ceiling where it had started as a black spot, growing till it reached the walls. Long black fingers began crawling down the four walls, and there they touched the other paintings and objects on those walls, the dark took their colours from them, they faded, became grey and then disappeared, swallowed up by the descending black shroud. As the unearthly darkness deepened, grew thicker as some abominable fog, the colours of the portrait seemed to sharpen, to radiate almost. It was as if the face of the girl began to spread a strange light of her own to counteract the growing darkness. Then he stepped inside the pentagram and spoke the last words. Only the big circle of the pentagram was lighted now, the room outside it seemed to have disappeared completely. It had been absorbed by thick string of almost material darkness, an obscurity which seemed in a frightful way to possess a private life, which seemed to be watching him constantly though it had no eyes.

He was looking at the painting. The very air around it seemed to shiver, as if acted upon by heat from some unknown source. Cenaide's face seemed to shrink until it was like a jewelled flower in the middle of a pulsating circle of black light. He stretched out his arms towards the shrinking face, and they seemed to grow and grow, his hands blossoming at their ends as alien flowers. Then her face expanded again, filling the whole picture. Her eyes were looking at him, blue shards of sparkling glass, burning with a deep fire which reached right through his head into his brain. He thought he saw himself approaching in those eyes, very small and distorted. As he was looking, the hidden fire came through her eyes, burst through her pupils and came swirling at him in threads of burning light, as a spider's web suddenly catching the sunlight of autumn and shining silvery. It exploded in all directions, beyond the pentagram, shivering as a silver maze, before the darkness outside absorbed it too.

It was as if the colours of the painting detached themselves from it, changing into alien, moving shapes of things for which there were no names, crawling and shrieking, blasphemous monstrosities moving inside the pentagram, before they too were taken by the darkness of the room. The darkness seemed closer, as if it was trying to edge inside the protecting pentagram; it was everywhere around him, circling him like a cocoon. Jack didn't notice it.

'I love you, Cenaide,' he whispered. Though spoken so softly, the words seemed an explosion of sound, repeating themselves through endless corridors, as if the dark rejected them and bounced them back along its inner walls. '... love you... love you...'

Only the portrait seemed to keep its reality, and the woman in it, who was looking at him, straight at him with her blue burning eyes. Then her lips parted, 'And I love you, Jack,' she said. The colours around her began to change, they seemed to melt though this was impossible, and dripped down from the canvas. Cenaide moved, slowly, deliberately, she stood up. The colours became a cloaking fog through which she came to him, slowly stretching her arms out. The colours were imploding in his brain, he couldn't think, could hardly react to what he saw and experienced. On the bare canvas, the silver pentagram was pulsating, emitting beams of an unearthly black light. The darkness around the greater pentagram was throbbing as with an immense heartbeat, and slowly the first fingers of the dark began crawling inside the pentagram. But he didn't see, didn't hear, except for the face coming to him, the face he had wanted so much, with the eyes burning fiercely into his own; the only clear thought in his mind was, 'God, if it is a dream, let it continue, let it never stop, if it isn't real it doesn't matter!' And then she was in his arms, soft, warm and very alive for the petrified shard of one second; he felt the silk of her hair, the softness of her parted lips as he kissed her, just before he tasted the bitter staleness of dry paint on his mouth.

After four continuous days of silence, they broke down the door of Jack Morgan's study, and found him, lying in the centre of his chalk-drawn pentagram, like a crucified spider. Paint was everywhere inside the pentagram, as if a madman, and who else could it have been but himself, had opened all his tubes and squeezed the paint in all directions. Most of it however, was on Jack Morgan himself, on his chest and arms and face, covering his eyes and nostrils completely, a thick mass of dried paint. There were severe burns on his face and hands as well, below the paint, but it was not this, nor suffocation which had killed him.

They buried him with the little savings they found in one of his drawers, among some records and old sketches; Cenaide wore a black veil and cried, but then she always had cried easily. There were also some friends, who said some nice words about him, though they would forget him before the year had passed. None of them could explain why the paint of what had been Cenaide's por-trait had run off the canvas as if completely fresh and fluent as water, so that except for some snatches of background detail, there now only stood a black glaring pentagram.

There was an official investigation, of course, but they came to a dead end when the coroner disclosed, baffled, that suffocation hadn't killed the painter. None of the experts was able to explain the murderous presence of thick quantities of paint inside his stomach, lungs, brain and heart.

THE SATYR'S HEAD

By David A. Riley

To turn and look upon its face,
Brought fear I'd never known -
The shadow has ever haunted me,
As I walk the earth so alone -

Karl Edward Wagner.

'C'est de Diable qui tient les fils qui nous remuent!
Aux objets repugnants nous trouvons des appas;
Chaque jour vers l'Enfer nous descendons d'un pas,
Sans horreur, a travers des tenebres qui puent.

'Serre, fourmillant, comme un million d'helmintnes
Dans nos cerveaux ribote up people le Demons,
Et, quand nous respirons, la Mort dans nos poumons
Descend, fleuve invisible, avec de sourdes plaints.'

Baudelaire. Les Fleurs du mal.

A S HENRY LAMSON looked from the gate of his brother's farm on the outskirts of Pire he noticed that someone was walking along the lane in his direction. Although it did nothing to disconcert him at the time, he did wonder, as he bid farewell to the silhouetted figures in the doorway, before setting off for his bus stop, why someone should have been coming back from the moors at this time of the night, especially when it had been pouring down with rain all day.

Shrugging his shoulders, Lamson pulled his raincoat collar up high about his neck against the drizzle and picked his way as carefully as he could between the puddles in the deeply rutted lane. He wished now, as his feet sank in the half hidden mud, that he had thought to bring a torch with him when he came on his visit, since the moon, though full, only faintly showed through the clouds, and the lane was for the most part in shadow.

Engrossed as he was in finding a reasonably dry route along the lane, he did not notice until a few minutes later, when the lights of his brother's farm had disappeared beyond the hedgerow, that the figure he had seen was nearing him quickly. Already he could hear his footsteps along the lane.

Petulantly pausing to disentangle a snapped thorn branch that had caught on his trouser leg, he turned to watch the hunched figure hobbling towards him. A threadbare overcoat of an indeterminate colour swayed from about his body. In one hand he grasped a worn flat cap, while the other was thrust in his overcoat pocket for warmth.

When he finally succeeded in freeing himself of the twig, Lamson made to continue on his way; the man was obviously nothing more than a tramp, and an old one at that. As he started off, though, he heard him call out in a cracked bellow that rose and died in one breath:

"Arf a mo' there!'

Irritated already at the drizzle that was soaking inexorably through his coat, Lamson sighed impatiently. As the tramp hurried towards him through the gloom, he slowly made out his bristly, coarse and wrinkled face, whose dirt-grained contours were glossy with rain.

The old man stumbled to a halt and raucously coughed a volley of phlegm on the ground. The pale grey slime merged in with the mud. Lamson watched him wipe his dribbling mouth with the top of his cap. Disgusted at the spectacle, Lamson asked him what was the matter.

'Are you feeling ill?' He hoped that he wasn't. The last thing he wanted was to be burdened with someone like this.

'Ill?' The old man laughed smugly. 'Ne'er 'ad a day's illness in my life. Ne'er!'

He coughed and spat more phlegm on the ground. Lamson looked away from it.

Perhaps mistaking the reason for this action, the tramp said: 'But I don't want to 'old you up. I'll walk alon' with you, if you don't mind me doin'. That's all I called you for. It's a lonely place to be by yoursel'. Too lonely, eh?'

Lamson was uncertain as to whether this was a question or not. Relieved that the man was at least not against continuing down the lane, he nodded curtly and set off, the old man beside him.

'A raw night, to be sure,' the old man said, with a throaty chuckle.

Lamson felt a wave of revulsion sweep over him as he glanced at the old man's face in the glimmering light of one of the few lamp-posts by the lane. He had never before seen anyone whose flesh gave off such an unnatural look of roughness. Batrachian in some indefinable way, with thick and flaccid lips, a squat nose and deeply sunken eyes, he had the appearance of almost complete depravity. Lamson stared at the seemingly scaly knuckles of his one bare hand.

'Have you come far?' Lamson asked.

'Far?' The man considered the word reflectively. 'Not really far, I s'ppose,' he conceded, with a further humourless chuckle. 'And you,' he asked in return, 'are you goin' far, or just into Pire?'

Lamson laughed. 'Not walking, I'm not. Just on to the bus stop at the end of the lane, where I should just about catch the seven fifty-five for the centre.' He looked across at a distant farm amidst the hills about Pire; its tiny windows stood out in the blackness like feeble fireflies through the intervening miles of rain. He glanced at his watch. Another eight minutes and his bus would be due. As he looked up, Lamson was relieved to see the hedgerow end, giving way at a junction to the tarmac road that ran up along the edge of the moors from Fenley. The bus shelter stood beside a dry-stone wall, cemented by Nature with tangled tussocks of grass. Downhill, between the walls and lines of trees, were the pin-pointed lines of streetlights etched across the valley floor. It was an infallibly awe-inspiring sight, and Lamson felt as if he had passed through the sullen voids of Perdition and regained Life once more.

On reaching the shelter he stepped beneath its corrugated roof out of the rain. Turning round as he nudged a half empty carton of chips to one side he saw that the man was still beside him.

'Are you going into Pire as well,' Lamson asked. He tried, not too successfully, to keep his real feelings out of his voice. Not only did he find the tramp's company in itself distasteful, but there was a foetid smell around him which was reminiscent in some way of sweat and of seaweed rotting on a stagnant beach. It was disturbing in that it brought thoughts, or half thoughts, of an unpleasant type to his mind. Apparently unaware of the effect he was having on Lamson, the tramp was preoccupied in staring back at the moors. Willows and shrubs were thrown back and forth in the gusts, intensifying his feelings of loneliness about the place.

Finally replying to Lamson's inquiry, the tramp said:

'There's nowhere else a body can go, is there? I've got to sleep. An' I can't sleep out in this.' His flat, bristly, toad-like head turned round. There was a dim yellow light in his eyes. 'I'll find a doss somewhere.'

Lamson looked back to see if the bus was in sight, though there were another four minutes to go yet before it was due. The empty expanse of wet tarmac looked peculiarly lonely in the jaundiced light of the sodium lamps along the road.

Fidgeting nervously beside him, the old man seemed to have lost what equanimity he'd had before. Every movement he made seemed to cry out the desire to be on his way once more. It was as if he was morbidly afraid of something on the moors behind him. Lamson was bewildered. What could there be on the moors to worry him? Yet, whether there was really something there for him to worry about or not, there was no mistaking the relief which he showed when they at last heard the whining roar of the double-decker from Fenley turning the last bend in the slope uphill, its headlights silhouetting the bristling shrubs along the road and glistening the droplets of rain. A moment later it drew up before them, comfortingly bright against the ice-grey hills and sky. Climbing on board, Lamson sat down beside the nearest window, rubbing a circle in the misted glass to look outside.

The tramp slumped down beside him.

He was dismayed when, in the smoke-staled air, the smell around the old man became even more noticeable than before, whilst his cold, damp body seemed to cut him off from the warmth he had welcomed on boarding the bus.

Apparently unconcerned by such matters, the tramp grinned sagaciously, saying that it was good to be moving once more. His spirits were blatantly rising and he ceased looking back at the moors after a couple of minutes, seemingly satisfied.

In an effort to ignore the foetor exuded by the man, Lamson concentrated on looking out of the window, watching the trees and meadows pass by as they progressed into Pire, till they were supplanted by the gardened houses of the suburbs.

"'Ave you a light?' The frayed stub of a cigarette was stuck between the tramp's horny fingers.

His lips drawn tight in annoyance, Lamson turned round to face him as he searched through his pockets. Was there to be no end to his intolerable bother? he wondered. His eyes strayed unwillingly about the scaly knuckles of the man's hand, to the grimily web-like flaps of skin stretched at their joints. It was a disgustingly malformed object, and Lamson was certain that he had never before seen anyone whose every aspect excited nothing so much as sheer nausea.

Producing a box of matches, he struck one for him, then waited while he slowly sucked life into his cigarette.

When he settled back a moment later, the tramp brought the large hand he had kept thrust deep in his overcoat pocket out and held it clenched before Lamson.

'Ever seen anythin' like this afore?' he asked cryptically. Like the withered petals of a grotesque orchid, his fingers uncurled from the palm of his hand.

Prepared as he was for some forgotten medal from the War, tarnished and grimy, with a caterpillar segment of wrinkled ribbon attached, Lamson was surprised when he saw instead a small but well-carved head of dull black stone, which looked as though it might have been broken from a statue about three feet or so in height.

Lamson looked at the tramp as the bus trundled to a momentary stop and two boisterous couples on a night out climbed on board, laughing and giggling at some murmured remark. Oblivious of them, Lamson let the tramp place the object in his hand. Though he was attracted by it, he was simultaneously and inexplicably repelled. There was a certain hungry look to the man's face on the broken head which seemed to go further than that of mere hunger for food.

Lamson turned the head about in his fingers, savoring the pleasant, soap-like surface of the stone.

'A strange thing to find out there, you'd think, wouldn't you?'

the old man said, pointing his thick black stub of a thumb back at the moors.

'So you found it out there?' Somehow there was just enough self-control in Lamson's voice to rob it of its disbelief. Though he would have wanted nothing more a few minutes earlier than to be rid of the man, he felt a yearning now to own the head himself that deterred him from insulting the tramp. After all, there was surely no other reason for the man showing the thing to him except to sell it. And although he had never before felt any intense fascination in archaeology, there was something about the head which made Lamson desire it now. He was curious about it as a small boy is curious about a toy he has seen in a shop window.

Intent on adding whatever gloss of credibility to his tale that he could, the old tramp continued, saying:

'It were in a brook. I found it by chance as I were gettin' m'self some water for a brew. It'd make a nice paperweight, I thought. I thought so as soon as I saw it. It'd make a nice paperweight, I thought.' He laughed self-indulgently, wiping his mouth with the sleeve of his coat. 'But I've no paper to put it on.'

Lamson looked down at the carving and smiled.

When the bus drew up at the terminus, Lamson was surprised, though not dismayed, when the tramp hurriedly climbed off and merged with the passing crowds outside. His bowlegged gait and crookedly unkempt figure were too suggestive of sickness and deformity for Lamson's tastes, and he felt more eager than ever for a salutary pint of beer in a pub before going on home to his flat.

Pressing his way through the queues outside the Cinerama on Market Street, he made for the White Bull, whose opaque doors swung open steamily before him with an out blowing bubble of warm, beery air.

One drink later, and another in hand, he stepped across to a vacant table up in a corner of the lounge, placing his glass beside a screwed-up bag of crisps.

A group of men were arguing amongst themselves nearby, one telling another, as of someone giving advice:

'A standing prick has no conscience.'

There was a nodding of heads and another affirmed: 'That's true enough.'

Disregarding them as they sorted out what they were having for their next round of drinks, Lamson reached in his pocket and brought out the head. A voice on the television fixed above the bar said:

'You can be a Scottish nationalist or a Welsh nationalist and no one says anything about it, but as soon as you say you' re a British nationalist, everyone starts calling out "Fascist!"'

Two of the men nodded to each other in agreement.

Holding the head in the palm of his hand, Lamson realized for the first time just how heavy it was. If not for the broken neck, which showed clearly enough that it was made out of stone, he would have thought it to have been molded from lead. As he peered at it, he noticed that there were two small ridges on its brows which looked as though they had once been horns

As he studied them, he felt that if they had remained in their entirety, the head would have looked almost satiric, despite the bloated lips. In fact, the slightly raised eyebrows and long, straight nose—or what remained of them—were still reminiscent of Pan.

He heard a glass being placed on the table beside him. When he looked up he saw that it was Allan Sutcliffe.

'I didn't notice you in here before. Have you only just got in?' Lamson asked.

Sutcliffe wiped his rain-spotted glasses on a handkerchief as he sat down, nodding his head. He replaced his glasses, then thirstily drank down a third of his pint before unbuttoning his raincoat and loosening the scarf about his neck. His face was flushed as if he had been running.

'I didn't think I'd be able to get here in time for a drink. I have to be off again soon to get to the Film Society. What have you got there, Henry? You been digging out your garden or something?'

Almost instinctively, Lamson cupped his hands about the head.

'It'd be strange sort of garden in a second floor flat, wouldn't it?' he replied acidly.

He drew his hands in towards his body, covering what little still showed of the head with the ends of his scarf. Somehow he felt ashamed of the thing, almost as if it was obscene and repulsive and peculiarly shameful.

'Where did you say you were off to?' he asked, intending to change the subject. 'The Film Society? What are they presenting tonight?'

'*Nosferatu*. The original. Why? D'you fancy coming along to it as well? It's something of a classic, I believe. Should be good.'

Lamson shook his head.

'Sorry, but I don't feel up to it tonight. I only stopped in for a pint or two before going on home and getting an early night. I've had a long day already, what with helping my brother, Peter, redecorating the inside of his farmhouse. I'm about done in.'

Glancing significantly at the clock above the bar, Sutcliffe drained his glass, saying, as he placed it back on the table afterwards: 'I'll have to be off now. It starts in another ten minutes.'

'I'll see you tomorrow as we planned,' Lamson said. 'At twelve, if that's still okay?'

Sutcliffe nodded as he stood up to go.

'We'll meet at the Wimpy, then I can get a bite to eat before we set off for the match.'

'Okay.'

As Sutcliffe left, Lamson opened his sweat-softened hands and looked at the head concealed in the cramped shadows in between. Now that his friend had gone, he felt puzzled at his reaction with the thing. What was it about the thing that should affect him like this? he wondered to himself. Placing it back in his pocket, he decided that he had had enough of the pub and strode outside, buttoning his coat against the rain.

Sunlight poured with a cold liquidity through his bedroom window when Lamson awoke. It shone across the cellophane that protected the spines of the hardbound books on the shelves facing his bed, obscuring their titles. It seemed glossy and bright and clean, with the freshness of newly fallen snow.

Yawning contentedly, he stretched, then drew his dressing gown onto his shoulders as he gazed out of the window. Visible beyond the roof opposite was a bright and cloudless sky. He felt the last dull dregs of sleep sloughing from him as he rubbed away the fine granules that had collected in his eyes. Somewhere he could hear a radio playing a light pop tune, though it was almost too faint to make out.

Halfway through washing he remembered the dreams. They had completely passed from his mind on wakening, and it was with an unpleasant shudder that they returned to him now.

The veneer of his cheerfulness was dulled by the recollection, and he paused in his ablutions to look back at his bed. They were dreams he was not normally troubled with, and he was loath to think of them now.

'To Hell with them!' he muttered self-consciously as he returned to scrubbing the threads of dirt from underneath his nails.

The measured chimes of the clock on the neo-Gothic tower, facing him across the neat churchyard of St. James, were tolling midday when Lamson walked past the Municipal Library. Sutcliffe, who worked at a nearby firm of accountants as an articled clerk, would be arriving at the Wimpy further along the street any time now. Going inside, Lamson ordered himself a coffee and took a seat by the window. He absent-mindedly scratched his hand, wondering nonchalantly, when he noticed what he was doing, if he had accidentally brushed it against some of the nettles that grew up against the churchyard wall. A few minutes later Sutcliffe arrived, and the irritation passed from his mind, forgotten.

'You're looking a bit bleary eyed today, Henry,' Sutcliffe remarked cheerfully. 'An early night, indeed! Too much bed and not enough sleep, that's your trouble.'

'I wish it was,' Lamson replied. 'I slept well enough last night. Too well, perhaps.'

'Come again?'

'Some dreams—' Lamson started to explain, before he was interrupted by Sutcliffe as the waitress arrived.

'Wimpy and chips and coffee, please.'

When she'd gone, Sutcliffe said: 'I'm sorry. What was that you were saying?'

But the inclination to tell him had gone. Instead, Lamson talked about the Rovers' chances this afternoon in their match against Rochdale. As they spoke, though, his mind was not wholly on what they were talking about. He was troubled, though he did not know properly why, by the dreams he had been about to tell Sutcliffe about, but which, on reconsideration, he had decided to keep to himself.

He was glad that he had a full day ahead of him, what with the football match this afternoon and a date with Joan at the Tavern tonight. Sutcliffe was taking his fiancé with them, and it promised to be an enjoyable evening for them all. He only wished that his relationship with Joan, who he had been going out with now for three months, wasn't so peculiarly Platonic. Whether this was his fault or hers, he did not know. A bit of both, he supposed, when he thought about it. Yet, if things did not improve very soon, he knew that their relationship, whatever his own inner feelings might be, would start to cool. Was this the cause of the dreams? he wondered, as he tried to concentrate on what Sutcliffe was saying. There did not seem to be any other reason he could think of at the moment that could account for them, and he decided that this must be it.

As Lamson walked home through the vaporous gloom beneath the old street lamps along Beechwood Avenue, after leaving Joan at her parents' home, his mind was deep in thought. It had been, as he had expected, an enjoyable evening, but only because of the new folk group they had been able to listen to at the Tavern. Joan had been no different than before: friendly and feminine in every way that he could wish, talkative—but not too much so—intelligent, amusing, and yet... and yet what was missing? Or was it him? What was it, he wondered, that made him feel so fatherly towards her, instead of the way in which at all other times he wished, even yearned, to be?

If not for the unexpected sound of someone slipping on the pavement some distance behind him, he would not have been brought out of his reverie until he reached Station Road and the last, short stretch to his flat. As it was, he half intentionally, half instinctively turned round to see if someone had fallen.

But all he glimpsed on the otherwise deserted avenue was the vague impression of someone merging hurriedly with the shadowy privet bushes midway between the feeble light of the lamp posts further back. So fleeting was the impression, though, that he would have taken it for the blurred motion of a cat that had raced across the avenue, but for the distinct recollection of something having slipped on the footpath.

For a moment or two he waited and watched in vain, certain that whoever or whatever hid in the gloom of the privet had not moved since he turned, and was only waiting for him to turn back again to emerge. It was disturbing, and he tried to play down his nervousness with the thought that it was probably only some kids playing an idiotic game of hide-and-seek in the dark. Unconvinced though he was by this explanation, it was substantial enough for him as an excuse to turn round with at least the pretense of indifference and continue on his way home. Even so, it was with a definite feeling of relief, however, when he reached Station Road, where the bright shop windows, neon signs and the passing cars and buses brought him back into reality. With more speed than he usually employed he strode along to the door leading into his flat and raced up the two flights of stairs to his rooms.

As he closed the door behind him he noticed the small black head he had bought from the tramp perched where he had left it on the dresser, its outline gleaming in the reflection of the streetlights outside.

It was looking towards him, crooked at an obtuse angle on its broken neck. He threw his overcoat onto the bed and stepped to the window to draw the curtains together before switching on the light. He felt at the radiator opposite his bed by the bookcase. It was just lukewarm.

As he stared morosely about the room, he wondered what had made him buy the head. What perverse attraction had struck him about it before had gone, and all he could see in it now was ugliness and decay. He picked it up. It wasn't as if he could legitimately claim he'd bought it out of some kind of archaeological interest. It was years since he'd last pottered in that subject at school, and what enthusiasm he may have once had for it had been lost to him long ago. For a moment he rubbed the small lumps on its brows, but he felt too tired suddenly to study it tonight. There was a nagging ache in his back and his arms felt stiff, while the rash-like irritation had returned to tingle on the back of his hands.

Lamson dropped the stone head back on the dresser and began to change into his pajamas. He felt too tired now to think or even place his clothes folded up, as he normally did, on the table beside his bed.

For a moment he struggled to keep awake, but he could not resist. He did not want to resist. All he wanted to do was to surrender himself, his body and soul, to the dull black nothingness of sleep.

Sleep quickly overcame him as he lay on his bed and closed his eyes.

And in his sleep he dreamed.

There was a wood in his dream, a great, deep, darkly mysterious wood that filled him with unease as he listened to its decrepit oaks groaning in the wind.

He stood before it alone. But he did not feel alone. He could sense something watching him malevolently from the gloomy depths of the wood.

The twilight passed into the darkness of night. Shadows glided silently through the trees, gathering as if to stare out at him with small, round, rubicund eyes. Or was it his own eyes playing tricks with the dark?

Then he saw something emerge from the waist high ferns, crawling on all fours across the ground. It was almost black, its naked flesh dry and coarse, strung tight about its jutting bones. Its legs, though hairless, were as the legs of a goat, whilst shrunken breasts, some twelve in number, hung limply from its chest. They swayed as it moved, its jaundiced eyes gleaming from the deep black depths of their sockets with a foul anticipation. There was a convulsive twitching in its long, thin, bony hands.

Unable to move, Lamson watched it crawl towards him. Its

penis was hard with lust, the dark nipples of its breasts enlarged and tight. Its lips were wet with overflowing saliva as it drew towards him.

Though partially human, it was hideously inhuman, a foul, unearthly, cacodaemoniacal Pan. Stiff black horns curved upwards from its brows; a scaled and rat-like tail flicked from its spine. He could see the mounting tension of its poised phallus.

He tried to scream.

With all his strength he tried to scream, to cry out and tear himself away from the hideous creature creeping towards him, but there was nothing he could do. He was paralyzed and defenseless.

A murmured chanting sibilantly issued encircling trees, flitting with the wind.

'Ma dheantar aon scriosadh, athru, gearradh, lot no milleadh ar an ordu feadfar diultu d'e a ioc.'

The rhythmic chanting began to mimic the frenzied beating of a heart, faster and deeper, as the satyr, swaying its lean torso to the rhythms of the chants, came upon Lamson. Its left hand grasped him about the thigh, pulling him down till he knelt on the ground. Its foetid breath blew hot into his face like the searing gusts of a newly opened furnace. He could see the wrinkles in its clammy flesh and the sores suppurating on its lips.

With renewed urgency he wrenched himself free and tried to roll out of its way across the grass. But before he even saw it move he felt its hands grasping him once more. He kicked out at it, whimpering. Its talons tore a deep gash in his trousers and its palm slid searchingly down his leg.

Once more he kicked.

With a slow deliberation it reached out for the buckle of his belt and ripped it free.

It was crouched over him, its softly repulsive underbelly almost touching his legs. In the feeble light its body seemed huge.

With a sudden exertion Lamson managed at last to emit a scream.

As its hand reached for him between his legs darkness sprang up about him like a monstrous whirlpool.

He felt dizzy and sick, shuddering with horror as he awoke, his body drenched with perspiration in the tangled blankets of his bed. At the same time he felt the final climax of an orgasm clasp hold of him.

He lay back and gasped, weak with the intensity of his ejaculation. He felt suddenly fouled, as if he'd been dragged through demoniacal cesspools of sin.

Nauseated, he looked across from his bed at the carving. Its coarse features seemed even more hideous to him now than before, and he did not doubt but that in some repulsively Freudian way its lecherous features—mirrored, as he now realized, on the demon creature of his nightmare—had influenced his sleeping mind. As he looked at it he found it difficult to understand how he had failed to notice the unclean lust rampant about its face before, like some infernal incubus roused by the harlots of Hell. As he washed himself clean a few minutes later he wondered if it would not be better to get rid of the head, to throw it away and forget it, and in doing so, hopefully, rid himself of the dreams.

Only once, while he dressed, did a discordant thought make him wonder if, perhaps, the dream wasn't connected in some way with his unsatisfactory relationship with Joan. But the two things were at such extremes in his mind that he could not connect them with anything other than shame. As he looked at the stone this shame transferred itself to this object, intensifying into a firm resolve to get rid of the thing. How could he possibly make any kind of headway with Joan, he told himself, with such a foul obscenity as that thing troubling him?

When Lamson left his flat a short time later, carrying the head in his raincoat pocket, it was with steps so unsteady that he wondered if he was coming down with something. The irritation on his hands had, if anything, become even worse, while aches and pains announced their presence from all over his body while he walked. He wondered if he had overstrained himself when he was helping his brother redecorate his farm, though he'd felt fit enough the day before. The Sunday morning streets were agreeably deserted as he walked along them. The only cars in sight were parked by the kerb. In a way he was glad that the dream had woken him as early as it had. Just past eight thirty now, it would be a while yet, he knew, before the city would start stirring into life today.

'Dirt-y o-old ma-an, dirty o-old ma-an!' He looked across to where the singsong voices came from. Two small boys of about ten or eleven years in age, perhaps less, were stood at the corner of the street in a shop doorway. Cheeky little brats, Lamson thought to himself as he noticed the shuffling figure their jeers were directed against, a stooped old man slowly making his way down a street leading off from the main road past a line of overfilled dustbins.

Although Lamson could not see his face he could tell that the old man knew the boys were calling out at him. Slow though his pace was, it was also unmistakably hurried, as if he was trying to get out of their way as quickly as he could on his old, decrepit legs.

'Clear off!' Lamson shouted angrily, feeling sorry for the old man.

The kids yelped and ran off down an alley, laughing.

If he had not felt so weary himself he would have run after them. How could they act so callously? He watched the old man as he continued up the street. There was something about the painful stoop of his back and the way his legs were bent, that struck a chord of remembrance somewhere. He could almost have been the tramp he met on the moors, except that he hadn't been anything like as decrepit as this man obviously was, not unless his health had failed disastrously over the last couple of days.

Lamson crossed the road and headed up past St. James church, putting the old man out of his mind. The pleasant singing of the birds in the elms that filled the churchyard helped to ease his spirits, and he breathed in the scent of the grass with a genuine feeling of pleasure. He only wished that his legs didn't feel so stiff and tired. He wondered again if he was coming down with a bug of some kind.

He paused suddenly by the wall and felt in his pocket, his fingers moving speculatively about the small stone head. Though he did not know properly why, he decided that the churchyard was too near his flat for him to get rid of the stone here. It would be better if he made his way to the canal where he could lose it properly without trace.

As he turned round to leave, he noticed a slight movement out of the corner of his eye. With a feeling of trepidation he paused, turned round and anxiously scanned the solemn rows of headstones.

Nothing moved, except for a light film of drizzle that began to filter down through the overhanging boughs of the trees. Yet, even though he could not see anything to account for what he seemed to have glimpsed, like a blurred shadow moving on the edge of his sight, he was sure that he was not mistaken. He stepped up the street to where a narrow gate led into the churchyard. He looked across it once again, and wished that he could make himself leave this suddenly disturbing place, but he could not. With slow, but far from resolute steps, he walked down the asphalt path between the headstones, his senses attuned to the least disturbance about him: the cold moisture of the drizzle on his hands and face, the hissing of the leaves as the rain passed through them, the singing of the birds that echoed and re-echoed about him, and the distant murmur of a car along Station Road as the clock tolled a quarter to nine. The air seemed strangely still. Or was it his own overwrought imagination, keyed up by the horrendous nightmare, scenes from which still flickered uncomfortably in front of him? He felt a fluttering sensation in his stomach as he looked along the roughhewn stones of the church with its incised windows of stained glass.

Quickening his pace, as the drizzle began to fall with more weight, he passed round the church. As he walked by the trees on the far side of the building, where they screened it off from the bleak back walls of a derelict mill, he again noticed something move. Was it a dog? he wondered, though it had seemed a little large. He whistled, though there was no response other than a thin, frail echo.

He strode between a row of ornate monuments of polished marble. Was that someone there, crouched in the bushes?

'Excuse me!' he called enquiringly. Then stopped. Calling out to a dog, indeed! he thought as he glimpsed what he took to be a large black hound—perhaps an Irish wolfhound—scutter off out of sight between the trees.

As he walked back to the street, he decided that it was about time he got on his way to the canal before the rain got any worse.

The rain did worsen. By the time he reached the towpath of the canal, he was beginning to regret having come out on a morning like this on such a pointless exercise. The rain covered the fields on either side of the canal in a dull grey veil. What colours there were had been reduced to such a washed-out monochrome that the scene reminded him of that in an old and faded photograph. Facing him across the dingy waters of the canal were rows of little sheds and barbed wire fences. Crates of neglected rubbish had been abandoned in the sparsely grassed fields, together with the tyreless carcasses of deserted cars. The fields rose up to the back of a grim row of tenements whose haphazard rooftops formed a jagged black line against the sky. Only the moldering wood of the derelict mills and their soot-grimed bricks on his side of the canal stood out with any clarity.

A dead cat floated in a ring of scum in the stagnant water at his feet, its jellied eyes sightlessly staring at the sky with a dank luminescence.

As he took the stone head from his pocket, Lamson heard someone move behind him. Having thought that he was safely alone, he spun round in surprise. Crouched deep in the shadows between the walls of the mill, where a gate had once stood, was a man. A long, unbuttoned overcoat hung from about his hunched body. It was a coat that Lamson recognized instantly.

'So it was you those kids were shouting at,' Lamson accused, as the tramp tottered out into the light. 'Have you been following me?' he asked. But there was no response, other than a slight twitching of the old man's blistered lips into what he took to be a smile, though one that was distinctively malignant and sly. 'You were following me last night, weren't you?' Lamson went on. 'I heard you when you slipped, so there's no point denying it. And I saw you this morning when those kids were having a go at you. I thought they were being cruel when they shouted out at you, but I don' t know now. Perhaps they were right. Perhaps you are a dirty old man, a dirty, insidious and evil old man.' Even now there was no more response from the tramp than that same repugnant smile. 'Haven't you got a tongue?' Lamson snapped. 'Grinning there like a Gargoyle. Well? You were talkative enough when we met on the moors. Have you taken vows of silence since then? Come on! Speak up, damn you!' He clenched his fists, fighting back the impulse to hit him in the face, even though it was almost too strong to resist. What an ugly old creature he was, what with his pockmarked face all rubbery and grey and wet, and those bloated, repulsive lips. Was he some kind of half-breed? he wondered, though of what mixture he could not imagine. A thin, grey trickle of saliva hung down from a corner of his mouth. There was a streak of blood in it. As he stared at him he realized that he looked far worse, far, far worse than before, as if whatever disease had already swollen and eroded his features had suddenly accelerated its effect.

The tramp stared down at the stone in Lamson' s hand.

'Were you after gettin' rid of it? Is that why you've come to this place?' he asked finally.

'Since it's mine, I have every right to, if that's what I want to do,' Lamson said, taken aback at the accusation.

'An' why should you choose to do such a thing, I wonder? You liked it enough when I first showed it to you on the bus. Couldn't 'ardly wait to buy it off o' me then, could you? 'Ere's the money, give us the stone, quick as a flash! Couldn't 'ardly wait, you couldn't. An' ere you are, all 'et up an' nervous, can't 'ardly wait to get rid o' the thing. What's the poor sod been doin' to you? Givin' you nightmares, 'as it?'

'What do you mean?'

'What should I mean? Just a joke. That's all. Can't you tell? Ha, ha, ha!' He spat a string of phlegm on the ground. 'Only a joke,' he went on, wiping his mouth with his sleeve.

'Only a joke, was it?' Lamson asked, his anger inflamed with indignation at the old man's ill-concealed contempt for him. 'And I suppose it was only a joke when you followed me here as well? Or did you have some other purpose in mind? Did you?'

'P'raps I was only tryin' to make sure you came to no 'arm. Wouldn't want no 'arm to come to you now, would I? After all, you bought that 'ead off o' me fair an' square, didn't you? Though it does seem an awful shame to me to toss it into the canal there. Awful shame it'd be. Where'd you get another bit o' stone like that? It's unique, you know, that's what it is right enough. Unique.

Wouldn't want to throw it into no canal, would you? Where's the sense in it? Or the use? Could understand if there was somethin' bad an' nasty about it. Somethin' unpleasant, like. But what's bad an' nasty about that? Don't give you no nightmares, now, does it? Nothin' like that? Course not! Little bit o' stone like that? An' yet, 'ere you are, all 'et up an' ready to toss it away, an' no reason to it. I can't understand it at all. I can't. I swear it.' He shook his head reproachfully, though there was a cunning grin about his misshapen mouth, as if laughing at a secret joke. 'Throwin' it away,' he went on in the same infuriatingly mocking voice, 'Ne'er would ha' thought o' doin' such a thing— old bit o' stone like that. You know 'ow much it might be worth? Can you even guess? Course not! An' yet you get it for next to nothin' off o' me, only keep it for a day or so, then the next thing I knows, 'ere you are all ready to toss it like an empty can into the canal. An' that's what you've come 'ere for, isn't it?'

'And if it is, why are you here?' Lamson asked angrily. The old man knew too much—far, far too much. It wasn't natural! 'What are you?' he asked. 'And why have you been spying on me? Come on, give me an answer!'

'An answer, is it? Well, p'raps I will. It's too late now, I can tell, for me to do any 'arm in lettin' you know. 'E's 'ad 'is 'ands on you by now, no doubt, Eh?'

Lamson felt a stirring in his loins as he remembered the dream he had woken from barely two hours ago. But the old man couldn't mean that. It was impossible for him to know about it, utterly, completely, irrefutably impossible! Lamson tried to make himself leave, but he couldn't, not until he had heard what the old man had to say, even though he knew that he didn't want to listen. He had no choice. He couldn't. 'Are you going to answer my questions?' he asked, his voice sounding far more firm than he felt.

The tramp leered disgustedly.

"Aven't 'ad enough, 'ave you? Want to 'ear about it as well?'
'As well as what?'
The tramp laughed. 'You know. Though you pretend that you
don't, you know all right. You know.' He wiped one watering, red-
rimmed eye. 'I 'spect you'll please 'im a might bit better 'n' me. For
a while, at least. I wasn't much for 'im, even at the first. Too old.
Too sick. Even then I was too sick. Sicker now, though, o' course.
But that's 'ow it is. That's 'ow it's got to be, I s'ppose. 'E wears you
out. That 'e does. Wears you out. But you, now, you, you're as
young as 'e could ask for. An' fit. Should last a while. A long, long
while, I think, before 'e wears you out. Careful! Wouldn't want to
drop 'im now, would you?'
It seemed as if something cold and clammy was clenching itself
like some tumorous hand inside him. With a shudder of revulsion,
Lamson looked down at the stone in his hand. Was he mistaken or
was there a look of satisfaction on its damnable face? He stared at
it hard, feeling himself give way to a nauseating fear that drained
his limbs of their strength.
'I thought you were o' the right sort for 'im when I saw you on
that lane,' the tramp said. 'I'm ne'er wrong 'bout things like that.'
As if from a great distance Lamson heard himself ask what he
meant.
'Right sort? What the fucking hell do you mean: the right sort?'
'Should ha' thought you'd know,' he replied, touching him on
the hand with his withered fingers.
Lamson jerked his hand away.
'You dirty old sod!' he snapped, fear and disgust adding tension
to his voice. 'You—you...' He did not want to face the things hinted
at. He didn't! They were lies, all lies, nothing but lies! With a
sudden cry of half hearted annoyance, both at the tramp and at
himself for his weakness, he pushed past and ran back along the
towpath. He ran as the rain began to fall with more force and the

sky darkened overhead. He ran as the city began to come to life and church bells tolled their beckoning chimes for the first services of the day.

'I can't understand you,' Sutcliffe said as he collected a couple of pints from the bar and brought them back to their table by the door. 'Excuse me,' he added, as he pushed his chair between a pair of outstretched legs from the next table. 'Right. Thanks.'

Loosening his scarf, he sat down with a shake of his tousled head.

'Like the Black Hole of Calcutta in here,' he said. He took a sip of his pint, watching Lamson as he did so. His friend's face looked so pale and lifeless these days, its unhealthiness emphasized by the dark sores that had erupted about his mouth.

'In what way can't you understand me?' Lamson asked.

There was a dispirited tiredness to his voice which Sutcliffe could tell didn't spring from boredom or disinterest.

Folding his arms, Sutcliffe leant over the table towards him.

'It's two weeks now since you last went out with Joan. And that was the night we all went to the Tavern. Since then nothing. No word or anything. From you... But Joan has called round to your flat four times this week, though you weren't apparently in. Unless you've found someone else you'd better know that she won't keep on waiting for you to see her. She has her pride, and she can tell when she's being snubbed. Don't get me wrong. I wouldn't like you to think I'm interfering, but it was Joan who asked me to mention this to you if I should bump into you. So, if you have some reason for avoiding her, I'd be glad if you'd let me know.' He shrugged, slightly embarrassed by what he'd had to say. 'If you'd prefer to tell me to mind my own bloody business I'd understand, of course. But, even if only for Joan's sake, I'd rather you'd say something.'

Suppressing a cough, Lamson wiped his mouth with a handkerchief, held ready in his hand. He wished he could tell Sutcliffe the reason why he was avoiding Joan, for a deliberate avoidance it was.

'I haven't been feeling too good recently,' he replied evasively.

'Is it anything serious?'

Lamson shook his head. 'No, it's nothing serious. I'll be better in a while. A bad dose of flu, that's all. But it's been lingering on.'

Sutcliffe frowned. He did not like the way in which his friend was acting these days, so unlike the open and friendly manner in which he had always behaved before, at least with him. Even allowing for flu, this neither explained the change in his character nor the peculiar swellings about his mouth. If it was flu, it was a flu of a far more serious nature than any he'd ever had himself. And how, for Christ's sake, could that explain the way in which his skin seemed to have become coarse and dry, especially about the knuckles on his hands?

'Have you been eating the right kinds of foods?' Sutcliffe asked. 'I know what it can be like living in a flat. Tried it once for a while. Never again! Give me a boarding house anytime. Too much like hard work for me to cook my own meals, I can tell you. I dare say you find it much like that yourself.'

'A little,' Lamson admitted, staring at his beer without interest or appetite as three men wearing election rosettes pressed by towards the bar. One of them said:

'I wouldn't be at all surprised if it wasn't something all these Asians have been bringing into the country. There's been an increase in TB already, and that was almost unheard of a few years ago.'

'It's certainly like nothing I've ever heard of, that's for sure,' one of the other two said.

As the men waited for their drinks, one of them turned round, smiling in recognition when he saw Lamson.

'Hello there. I didn't notice you were here when we came in.'

'Still working hard, I see,' Lamson said, nodding at the red, white and blue National Front rosette on the man's jacket.

'No rest for the wicked. Someone's got to do the Devil's work,' the man joked as the other two smiled in appreciation of his joke. 'It's the local elections in another fortnight,' he added.

Collecting their drinks, the men sat down at the table beside Lamson and Sutcliffe.

'I overheard you talking about TB. Has there been a sudden outbreak or something?' Lamson asked.

'Not TB,' the man said. 'We've just been talking to an old woman who told us that a tramp was found dead in an alleyway near her house earlier this week. From what we were able to gather from her, even the ambulance men themselves, who you'd think would be pretty well-hardened to that kind of thing, were shaken by what they saw.'

'What was it" Sutcliffe asked. 'A mugging?'

'No,' Reynolds—the man who had spoken—said with a dull satisfaction. 'Apparently he died from some kind of disease. They're obviously trying to keep news about it down, though we're going to try to find out what we can about it. So far there's been no mention in the press, though the local rag—*Billy's Weekly Liar*—isn't acting out of character there, especially with the elections coming up. So, just what it is we don't know, though it must be serious. Sickening, is how the old woman described him, though how she got a look at him is anybody's guess. But you know what these old woman are like. Somehow or other she managed to get a bloody good look—too good a look, I think, for her own peace of mind in the end! According to what she told us there were swellings and sores and discolourations all over his body. And blood dripping out of his mouth, as if his insides had been eaten away.'

Lamson shuddered.

'What's the matter?' Sutcliffe asked as he lit a cigarette.

Lamson smiled weakly.

'Just someone stepping over my grave, that's all,' he said. He took a long drink of his beer as the three men drained theirs. Putting his glass down, empty, Reynolds stood up. 'We'd better be off back to our canvassing or someone'll be doing a clog dance on our graves. And we'll be in them!'

As the men left, Lamson said that he could do with a whisky.

'Just because of what you heard about some poor old sod of a tramp?' Sutcliffe asked.

'It's not him,' Lamson replied. 'God help his miserable soul, but he was probably better off dead anyway.' Though what he said was meant to sound offhand, his voice lacked the lightness of tone to carry it off successfully. Realizing this, he pushed his glass away. 'I'm sorry—I must seem like poor company tonight. I think it would perhaps be better if I set off home. Perhaps we'll meet up again tomorrow night? Yes?'

'If you say so,' Sutcliffe replied amicably. 'You do look a bit under the weather tonight.' A Hell of a lot under the weather, he added silently to himself. 'Anyhow, now that you mention it, it's about time I was on my way as well. I'll walk along with you to my bus stop. It's on your way.'

As they stepped out of the pub, Sutcliffe asked if he had been sleeping well recently.

'What makes you ask?'

'Your eyes,' Sutcliffe said as the wind pushed against them, a torn newspaper scuttering along the gutter. 'Red-rimmed and bleary. You ought to get a few early nights. Or see if your doctor can prescribe some sleeping pills for you. It's probably what you need.'

Lamson stared down the road as they walked along it. How cold and lonely it looked, even with the cars hissing by through puddles of rain, and the people walking hurriedly along the pavement. There was a smell of fish and chips and the pungent aroma of curry as they passed a takeaway, but even this failed to make him feel at home on the street. He felt foreign and lost, alienated to the things and places which had previously seemed so familiar to him. Even with Sutcliffe he felt almost alone, sealed within himself.

As they parted a few minutes later at Sutcliffe's stop outside the Unit Four on Market Street, his friend said:

'I'll be expecting you tomorrow. You've been keeping far too much to yourself recently. If you don't watch out you'll end up a hermit, and that's no kind of fate for a friend of mine. So mind you're ready when I call round. Okay?'

Lamson said that he would be. There was no point in trying to evade him. Sutcliffe was too persistent for that. Nor did he really want to evade him, not deep down. He pulled his coat collar up high about his neck and started off purposefully for his flat.

There was a gloom to his bedroom which came from more than just an absence of light, since even during the day it was there. It was a gloom which seemed to permeate everything within it like a spreading stain. As soon as Lamson stepped inside he was aware of the gloom, in which even the newest of his possessions seemed faded and cheap.

He looked at the stone head.

It drew his attention almost compulsively. Of everything it was the only object in the room that had not been affected by this strange malaise. Was it gloating? he wondered. Gloating at the way in which it had triumphed over everything else in the flat, including (or especially) the framed photo of Joan, with her blond hair curled so characteristically about her face? You're trapped with me, it seemed to say like some grotesque spider that had caught him on its dusty web, smirking and sneering with its repulsively hybrid, goatlike features. Lamson rubbed his hands together vigorously, trying to push the thoughts out of his mind. I must get rid of the thing, he told himself (as he had continually done, though without result, for the past two weeks).

He glanced at his unmade bed with distaste and a feeling of shame.

'Oh, God,' he whispered self-consciously, 'if only I could get rid of the obsession. Because that is all it is. No more. Only an obsession, which I can and must somehow forget.' Or was it? There was no way in which he could get away from the doubt. After all, he thought, how could he satisfactorily explain the way in which the tramp had seemed able to read his thoughts and know just what it was that he'd dreamed? Or was he only a part of this same single-minded and delusive obsession? he wondered, somewhat hopefully, as his mind grew dull with tiredness. He glanced at his watch. How much longer could he fight against falling asleep? One hour? Two? Eventually, though, he would have to give in. It was one fight, as he so well knew by now, which no one could win, no matter how much they might want to, or with how much will.

In an effort to concentrate his thoughts he picked out a book from the shelf randomly. It was *Over the Bridge* by Richard Church. He had quite enjoyed reading it once several months ago, but the words did not seem to have any substance in his brain anymore. Letters, like melting figures of ice, lost form and swam and merged as if the ink was still wet, and slowly soaking through the pages as he watched.

When, as was inevitable, he finally lost consciousness and slept, he became aware of a change in the atmosphere. There was a warmth which seemed womb-like and wrong in the open air. It disturbed him as he looked up at the stars prickling the sky, the deep, black, canopied darkness of the sky.

On every side trees rose from the gloom, their boughs bent over like thousands upon thousands of enormous, extended fingers, black in their damp decay. Their leaves were like limpets, pearly and wet, as they shivered in the rising winds.

Before him a glade led down beneath the trees.

Undecided as to which way he should go, Lamson looked about himself uncertainly, hoping for a sign, for some indication—however faint or elusive—as to which path was the one he should take. There seemed to be so many of them, leading like partially erased pencil lines across a grimy sheet of paper through the over-luxuriant grass. Somewhere there was a sound, though it was so dimmed and distorted by the distance separating him from its source. Sibilantly, vaguely, the rhythmic words wound their ways between the trees.

Finding himself miming them, he turned his back to the sounds and started for the glade. Even as he moved he knew that he had made a mistake. But he knew, also, with a sudden, wild wrenching of his heart, that there was no escape. Not now. It was something which he knew had either happened before or was preordained, that no matter what he did there was no way in which he could escape from what was going to happen next. He felt damned—by God, the Devil and himself.

Crestfallen, as the awfulness of what he knew was about to happen next came over him, he felt a sudden impulse to scream. Something large and heavy rustled awkwardly through the ferns. Fear, like lust, swelled within him. He felt a loathing and a horror and, inexplicably, a sense of expectation as well, almost as if some small part of him yearned for what it knew was about to take place. He began to sob. How could he escape from this thing—how could he possibly even hope to escape from this thing—if some perverse element within him did not want him to be free?

He turned round to retrace his steps up the glade, but there was something dark stretched across his path, barring his way, some yards ahead of him. It turned towards him and rose. Starlight, filtering through the trees, glittered darkly across its teeth as it smiled.

Lamson turned round and tried to run back down the glade, but the creature was already bounding after him like a great black goat. He felt its claws sink into his shoulders as it forced him forwards, knocking him suddenly face down onto the ground. He tried to scream, but his cries were gagged on dried leaves and soil, as his mouth was gouged into them. The creature's furiously powerful fingers tore at his clothes, strewing them about him. The winds blew cool against his hot, bare flesh as sweat from the lunging, piston-like body ran down the hollow of his spine.

There was a crash somewhere and the dream ripped apart.

The next instant he seemed to blink his eyes open to find the comforting sight of his familiar bedroom in front of him. The book he had been reading when sleep overcame him earlier, lay against his feet on the floor.

He breathed out a sigh of relief as he glanced at his watch. It was three thirty-five in the morning.

He shivered. Covered in sweat, his body felt awful, aching in every joint. He put on his dressing gown and crossed to the window, opening the curtains to look down into the twilit street below. It was empty and quiet, peaceful as it never was during the day. But it was also undeniably lonely. Cold and lonely and lifeless. The sight of its bleak, grey lines could not make him forget the dream for long, nor keep him away from the wretched feeling of despair that remembering it brought along with it, a despair made all the more unbearable at the realisation that its cause, deep down, must lie rooted in his character. There was no way in which he could deny to himself the perverted aspects it presented to him. But was he perverted as well? Or had the old tramp been lying? After all, he reasoned, why should he be any more perceptive of that kind of thing than anyone else? It was the man's horrible suggestion, and that was all—no more certainly!—that was making his mind work in that direction now. Almost, he thought, pensively staring about his room, like some kind of post hypnotic suggestion. And if this were so and it was the tramp's vile insinuations that had caused this neurotic and evil obsession, then it was up to him to vent these desires in the most normal way that he could. Otherwise, he knew, they would only worsen, just as they were worsening already.

Decided on this course, he rested quietly for the rest of the night, reading through the next few chapters of *Over the Bridge*, and listening to the radio.

When the sky began to lighten at last he welcomed the new day with a fervor he had not felt for many weeks. At last it seemed to him as if there was a chance of ridding himself of this nightmare.

At last...

It was not till midday that he dressed and stepped outside.

In realising that he had to prove to himself that he was normal, and rid himself of the perverse obsession that was deranging him, he had decided that the easiest way open to him was to call on Clara Sadwick, a local prostitute who rented rooms on Park Road above a newsagent's shop. As he walked towards it down the sodden street the place appeared to have a dingy and slightly obscene look to it, with unpainted window frames and faded curtains, pulled together tight behind their grimy, flyspecked windows.

As he stepped inside and began to climb the bare staircase to the first floor landing, he gazed bleakly at the mildewed paper on the walls. A naked light bulb swayed on the end of a cord at the head of the stairs. He wondered what he had let himself in for at a place like this. Fortifying himself, however, with the thought that in going through with what was to follow he might end the dreams that had been tormenting him for the past three weeks, he pressed on the buzzer by the door facing him at the top. One fifteen, she had said on the phone when he rang her an hour before. It was just a minute off that time now. He ran his fingers nervously through his uncombed hair.

After a short pause the door opened before him.

'Believe in punctuality, don't you?' Clara said with an offhand familiarity which made him feel more relaxed as she stepped back and looked at the slim gold watch on her wrist. She was dressed in a denim skirt, fluffy red slippers and a purple, turtle-necked sweater, which clung, about her ample breasts.

She smiled as she showed him in.

'Make yourself at home,' she said breezily.

'Thank you,' Lamson said as he hung his coat on a hook by the door and looked about the room. In the far corner, partially hidden behind a faded Japanese screen, was a bed. In front of the old gas fire stood a coffee table crammed with dirty plates. He wondered if she had been having a party or whether, as seemed dismayingly more likely, she merely washed them up when there were no more clean ones left. He hoped, fleetingly, that she was a little more conscientious about cleaning herself.

Clara ground the cigarette she'd been smoking into a saucer, then said:

'It'll be forty quid. Cash first, if you don't mind. It's not that I don't trust you, but 1 can hardly take you to court if you refuse to pay afterwards.'

Lamson smiled to cover his embarrassment, and said that he understood.

'You can't be too careful, can you?' he added, sorting out the notes from his wallet. 'Forty pounds, you said?' he went on, as he placed the money in her waiting hand.

'Many thanks,' she replied, taking it to a drawer and locking it inside.

She looked back at him coyly.

'Well, I suppose we had better begin,' she said, folding back the screen from the bed. With no further words, she kicked off her slippers and began to unbutton her skirt. Within a few minutes she was dressed only in her tights and bra. She looked up then as if only just remembering his presence, and told him to hurry. 'I haven't all day to wait for you getting undressed. Unless, of course, you prefer having it with your clothes still on.' She shook her head, laughing almost like a young girl, though she was in her late thirties, unfastening her bra and letting it fall forward from her breasts. Lamson swallowed as he stared at the limpid mounds of pale white flesh that were uncovered, their puckered orbs matching the goose flesh that was starting to rise on her cozily rounded arms.

She shivered, complaining to him again at his slowness.

'Do you want me to help you?' she asked sarcastically.

Lamson shook his head as he loosened his trousers and let them fall, unaided, to the floor. Stepping out of them onto the lukewarm oilcloth he looked at her again.

'Come on, luv,' she said as she rolled back on the rumpled bed. 'Off with the rest of them and we can begin.'

Although Lamson felt embarrassed at his nakedness as he slipped out of the last of his clothes, and could feel the blood burning through his cheeks, he was surprised—and not just a little alarmed—that there was no other reaction, that he seemed, in fact, to be incapable of carrying out what he had paid for. Seemingly unaware of this—or, if she was, taking no apparent notice of it— she smiled as he approached her. Lightly, questingly, her hands felt about his body as he pushed his face into her breasts. He smelt the faint aroma of sweat and eau-de-cologne, his mind whirling with haphazard and conflicting sensations. She pressed his mouth against her hardening nipples as he moved further up her body. Yet, still, he could not find the desire to possess her.

'Come on, come on, dearie,' he heard her whisper between gasps. He raised himself onto his elbows and looked down into her face. In the same instant her hands grasped hold of him between his legs. He gasped as her fingers lengthened and tightened gently about his penis, guiding him towards her. It was as if his loins were being instilled with a surcharge of life.

He looked down at her eyes—Joan's face seemed to merge with hers, hiding the cheapness and vulgarity that had been there a moment before. It was almost angelic. Never before had he looked upon a face such as this, upon which all his pent up emotions of warmth, affection and even love could be gladly poured. His eyes passed lingeringly about her warm, soft cheeks where the blood made a pleasant suffusion of pink. She smiled encouragingly, and yet with an apparent innocence which drove him into an almost unbearable desire to possess her. He felt her thighs rise on either side of his legs, pressing him to her. He could feel himself grow stiff, entering her slowly, cautiously passing into the warmth within her summoning body. He could have cried out at the exquisite pangs that were racing through him, obliterating conscious thought.

Even through the pleasure that was overwhelming his mind, though, Lamson became suddenly aware that the room was darkening. Something sharp and dry scraped painfully across his back. He cried out in alarm as it stuck, like a vicious hook, ruthlessly dragging him away from her.

The pain crescendoed suddenly as he was tugged from the bed and flung onto the floor. Contorted in agony, he looked up. He glimpsed something dark stride over him. There was a scream. It seemed to cut deep into his ears like slivers of glass, and he tried desperately to crawl back onto his knees. Then the screaming stopped, as suddenly as it began. Instead there was a ripping sound, like something being torn apart.

'No! God, no!' he sobbed, dizzy with nausea, his sight blurring as he seemed to start falling in a faint. Whatever stood over him still moved, its weight shifting from one leg to the other in sickening, horrifying rhythm to the rips and tears from the bed.

Feebly Lamson tried to reach out across the sheets to stop whatever was going on there, when something soft and warm touched his fingers.

Something wet.

It clung to him as he automatically recoiled away from it, screaming hysterically as darkness closed in all about him.

It could have been hours, or even just minutes afterwards, when he opened his eyes once more. However long he'd been unconscious, the tawdry bedchamber had gone, as if he had never been there. Instead he was stretched out on the floor of his flat, facing the window. A blowfly buzzed aggressively, though without result, against the windowpane. Besides this there was silence.

As he slowly climbed to his feet, his first reaction was one of intense relief. He could have laughed out loud in that one brief instant in joy at the fact that it had never happened, that it was all just a horrible dream, that he had never even left his flat!

Then he noticed the spots of blood on his shirt. There were scabs of it clotted about his hands and fingers. His stomach heaved with revulsion as he stared down at the ugly stains covering him like the deadly marks of a plague.

'Oh, my God!' he muttered, rushing convulsively to the sink to wash them from him. His hands still dripping, he grabbed hold of his shirt and tugged it from him, grinding his teeth against the pain in his back as the scabs swathed across it were torn open. His shirt had been glued to him by them. When the pain subsided enough for him to touch them, he gingerly felt across his back, his fingers cautiously trembling along the blood-clogged grooves gouged into him. Crestfallen with horror, he stared at his haggard face in the mirror above the sink. Did it happen? Was it not just a dream but some vile distortion of reality?

He stepped back into his bedroom and looked at the head, perched where he had left it. The thing stared at him with its coal-black, swollen eyes. It seemed bigger than before, like an oversized, blackened grapefruit. You know, he thought suddenly, you know what happened, you black swine of a devil! But no, this was madness. How could he believe that the thing had some sort of connection with what had happened? It must be something else. But what? he wondered. What but something equally bizarre, equally preposterous could account for it?

What?

What?

Outside he heard the two-tone siren of a police car as it sped down the road. After it had gone there was another. Lamson strode to the window and looked down as an ambulance hurtled by, its blue light blinking furiously.

He leant against the windowsill, feeling suddenly weak. Resignedly, he knew that it happened, it really did happen. By now they must have found her blood-soaked body, or what was left of it. He gazed down at the stains still sticking to his fingers, and wondered what he could do. Like the Brand of Cain, threads of blood clung to the hardened scales about his knuckles. If only he had thrown that stone away when he'd intended to originally. If he had, he was sure that none of this would have ever happened. He grabbed hold of the stone, clenching it tightly as if to crush it into dust. Something black seemed to move on the edge of his sight. He turned round in surprise, but there was nothing there now.

He placed the head back on the dresser and took a deep breath to compose himself. He wondered if he had left it too late to get rid of the head. Or was there time yet? After all, there was no saying what the thing might make him do next. Reluctantly, he looked again at the head. How he wished he could convince himself that it was nothing more than just an inanimate lump of stone. Once more he picked it up, his fingers experiencing the same kind of revulsion he would have felt on touching a diseased piece of flesh.

'Damn you,' he whispered tensely, suddenly flexing his arm. There was a movement by his side, furtive and vague. He whipped round. 'Where are you hiding?' he asked shakily, searching round the empty room. There seemed to be a sound somewhere, like the clattering of hoofs. Or was there? It echoed metallically, almost unreal. 'Come on, now, where are you hiding?' Something touched his arm. He cried out inarticulately in revulsion. 'Go away!' he choked, retreating to the window. He turned round to look outside, raising his hand and glancing at the head clasped tightly in his fingers.

Steady, now, steady, he told himself. Don't lose your grip altogether.

He coughed harshly, feeling the phlegm in his throat. It involuntarily dribbled from his lips and spilt on the floor. Looking down, he saw a string of blood in it. He closed his eyes tightly. He knew what it meant, though he wished fervently that he could believe that it didn't. He wished that he could have known earlier what he knew now and done then what he was about to do, when it wasn't already too late.

'God help me!' he cried as he tugged his arm free of the fingers that plucked at him, and flung the stone through the window. There was a crash as the glass was shattered, and he fell to the floor.

Something rose up above him, seeming monstrously large in the gloom of his faltering sight.

'Are you going up to see Mr. Lamson?' the elderly woman asked, detaining Sutcliffe with a nervously insistent hand.

'I am,' he replied. 'Why? Is there something wrong?' He did not try to hide his impatience. He was nearly half an hour late already.

'I don' t know,' she said, glancing up the stairs apprehensively. 'It was late this afternoon when it happened. I was cleaning the dishes after having my tea when I heard something crash outside. When I looked I found there was broken glass all over the flagstones. It had come from up there,' she pointed up the stairs, 'from the window of Mr. Lamson's flat; his window had been broken.'

His impatience mellowing into concern, Sutcliffe asked if anyone had been up to see if he was all right.

'Do you know if he's been hurt? He hasn't been too well recently and he might be sick.'

'I went up to his rooms, naturally,' the woman said. 'But he wouldn't answer his door. On no account would he, even when I called out to him, though he was in there right enough. I could hear him, you see, bumping around inside. Tearing something up, I think he was. Like books, I s'ppose. But he wouldn't open the door to me. He wouldn't even talk. Not one word. There was nothing more I could do, was there?' she apologized. 'I didn't know he was ill.'

'That's all right,' Sutcliffe said, thanking her for warning him. 'I'll be able to see how he is when I call up. I'm sure he'll answer his door to me when I call to him. By the way,' he went on to ask, turning round suddenly on the first step up the stairs, 'do you know what it was that broke the window?'

'Indeed I do,' the woman said. She felt in the pocket of her apron. 'I found this on the pavement when I went out to clear up the glass. It's been cracked, as you can see.' She handed him the stone. 'Ugly looking thing, isn't it?'

'It certainly is.' Sutcliffe felt at the worn features on its face. It was pleasantly soap-like and warm. He wondered why Lamson should have thrown something like this through his window. 'Do you mind if I hold onto it for a while?' he asked.

'You can keep it for good for all I care. I don't want it. I'm certain of that, Lord knows! It'd give me the jitters to keep an evil-looking thing like that in my rooms.'

Thanking her again, Sutcliffe bounded up the stairs, three at a time. He wondered worriedly if Lamson had thrown it through the window as a cry for help. Just let me be in time if it was, he thought, knocking on his door. 'Henry! Are you in there? It's me, Allan. Come on, open up!'

There was no sound.

Again he knocked, louder this time.

'Henry! Open up, will you?' Apprehensively, he waited an instant more, then he took hold of the door handle, turning it. 'Henry, I'm coming in. Keep well away from the door.' Heavily, he lunged against the door with his shoulder. The thin wood started to give way almost at once. Again he lunged against it, then again, then the door shot open, propelling Sutcliffe in with it.

'Where are you, Henr—' he began to call out as he steadied himself, before he saw what lay curled against the windowsill. Shuddering with nausea, Sutcliffe clasped a hand to his mouth and turned away, feeling suddenly sick. Naked and almost flayed to the bone, with tears along his doubled back, Lamson was crouched like a grotesque foetus amongst the blood-soaked tatters of his clothes. His head was twisted round, and it was obvious that his neck had been broken. But it was none of this, neither the mutilations nor the gore nor the look of horror and pain on Lamson's rigidly contorted face, that were to haunt him in the months to come, but an expression that lay raddled across his

:iend's dead face which he knew should have never been there—a ɔok of joyful ecstasy. And there was a hunger there, too, but a hunger that went further than that of mere hunger for food.